Dear George
and other stories

HELEN SIMPSON

Dear George

and other stories

HEINEMANN : LONDON

First published in Great Britain 1995
by William Heinemann Ltd
an imprint of Reed Consumer Books Ltd
Michelin House, 81 Fulham Road, London SW3 6RB
and Auckland, Melbourne, Singapore and Toronto

Permission to quote from *The First Six Months* by Penelope
Leach is given by Fontana, an imprint of HarperCollins
Publishers Limited

A CIP catalogue record for this title
is available from the British Library
ISBN 0 434 00044 2

Typeset by Deltatype Ltd, Ellesmere Port, Cheshire
Printed and bound in Great Britain
by Mackays of Chatham plc, Kent

Contents

Dear George

She was trying to write an essay on the various sorts of humour in *As You Like It* at the same time, which didn't help. To her right was a pad of file paper on which she scrawled scathing comments about Shakespeare as they occurred. In front of her was her mother's block of Basildon Bond. She had used four sheets so far.

Dear George, she wrote for the fifth time, and added a curly little comma like a tadpole. She sat back and admired the comma. That was pure luck when it turned out like that. Sometimes if you concentrated on something too hard you ruined it.

She sauntered over to the mirror and stared at herself for a few minutes. 'You gorgeous creature you,' she murmured, sly but sincere, ogling herself from sideways on. A yawn overtook her and she watched her tongue arch like a leaf. Then she performed a floozie's bump and grind back to the *Complete Works*.

Jaq: What stature is she of?
Orl: Just as high as my heart.

1

George was tall, that was the best thing about him. She would be higher than his heart, of course, probably about level with his Adam's apple, but that was good enough for her. Already her feet were seven-and-a-halfs, and she was still not yet fifteen.

She turned back to her latest copy of the letter to George. She knew its phrases by heart now, and they were as spontaneous as two hours' effort could make them. 'Daniel Minter asked me to tell you that the Grindley match has been rearranged for the 16th because he thought you were coming back to the Bio Lab, but you didn't. So I thought I'd drop you a line to let you know. He asked me because I had to be there till five o'clock on the last day of term, collecting the results from our petri dishes.'

The handwriting was vital, that was what she was trying to perfect as she toiled over copy after copy. There must be nothing round or childish about it. She was dabbling now with italics like barbed wire. Sophistication was what she aimed for. A looped *f* would still creep in if she didn't watch it, or a silly swan-backed *s*.

There was her fat little sister, rattling the doorknob to be let in.

'I won't talk,' came the promises through the keyhole. 'I'll just sit on your bed and watch you.'

'Go away,' she drawled. 'You are banal.'

Silence. She thought of her sister's big baffled sheep's eyes and this made her giggle crossly and feel cruel.

'Banal!' she bellowed. 'Look it up in the dictionary.'

Her sister rushed heftily off downstairs towards the bookcase. From another part of the house drifted a weak howl from their mother, who was trying to get the new baby to sleep.

Disgust jerked her out of her seat. How *could* she, at *her* age, it was so *selfish* of her. It was just showing off. As everyone at school had pointed out, she'd probably been trying for a boy this time, so *served her right*.

She would never be able to bring George home. It would be too awful. Her mother would probably try to breastfeed it in front of him. She started to wriggle and giggle in horror.

> Cel: I pray you, bear with me, I cannot go no further.
> Tou: For my part, I had rather bear with you than bear
> you: yet I should bear no cross if I did bear you,
> for I think you have no money in your purse.

She picked up her pen and scribbled, 'This is obviously meant to be funny, but it is not. It is rubbish. People only say this is good because it is Shakespeare. It is really boring. It is not even grammar, e.g. I cannot go no further.' The hexagonal plastic shaft of the biro turned noisily in the grip of her front teeth as she paused to read through what she had written. Then she crossed out 'boring' and printed 'banal' in its place.

'Commonplace. Trite. Hackneyed,' came through the keyhole with a lot of heavy breathing; then a pause and, 'What do *they* mean?'

'Go away,' she said. 'Ask Mum.'

Served her mother right if she used up all the stamps and Basildon Bond. Spitefully she folded and inserted each of the four early drafts into separate envelopes, sealed them and wrote out George's address four times with self-consciously soppy relish. She had no intention of sending any of them, and stuck on the stamps in a spirit of wicked waste. Later today she would tear them up to show she had style, and send off this perfect fifth version.

She read it through again. It was making her cringe now, she couldn't see it fresh any more. She'd read those phrases so often, she couldn't tell whether they came across as casual or childish or too keen or what.

'I wish I was in 6B with you, all the O-levels out of the way. Hope you have a good holiday. If you would possibly feel like meeting for any reason, I am fairly free this holiday. Maybe hear from you soon. Ciao.'

Was ciao too trendy? She hadn't thought it was till this moment. She couldn't put Yours sincerely, and shook at the thought of Love. Cheers was what the boys in 6B said to each other, but she wouldn't stoop that low.

'Dear George,' she scribbled again, this time on a naughty impulse and a sheet of scrap paper, 'I don't know I could stand to go out with you if Every Time We Said Goodbye you said Chiz instead. Why do you do it? It makes you sound really thick. Chiz chiz chiz chiz chiz. Try Ciao, it's more stylish – it's Italian in case you didn't know and it means the same as chiz – you look a bit Italian which is partly why I fancy you.'

The mournfulness of his image caught her, stopped her ticking for a second or two as a cameo of large meaty nobility filled her mind's eye.

She reread what she had written, then, sniggering, clattering her teeth together in enamelled applause, dipping her head down so that her hair piled up on one side of the paper in a foresty rustle, she scrawled, 'You can't be *that* thick. Anyone can have bad luck in O-levels, ha ha, though two retakes in history is a bit much.'

Cupping her chin on the half shell of her hands, she made her mouth into a kissing shape. With the tip of her tongue she tenderly tapped inside each of the teeth in her upper jaw.

'I would like to feel your hands on the back of my waist (25"), with the thumbs round my sides,' she scrawled, chewing invisible gum, 'but only if they aren't sweaty. If you have wet hands it's all over before it's started, sorry Gorgeous George but that's the way I am.'

Holding her hands up in front of her, using them like boned fans to block the light, she spotted an incipient hangnail poking up from the cuticle of her left thumb and fell on it like a falcon, tearing at it with famished energy. When she had made it bleed she lost interest and stared out of the window.

There on the back lawn her galumphing little sister was helping their mother hang out baby vests and babygros and other baby rubbish in the sun. Her mother had it strapped to her front in a hideous pink nylon sling.

'No style,' she muttered, curling her lip. She pulled the curtains on them and made a warm gloom.

Once the candle was lit and positioned on her homework table, she was able to ignore the worst aspects of her room, like the brainlessly 'cheerful' duvet cover with its sun, moon and poppy field. Her face's reflection was a blanched heart in the mirror on the back wall. When she came home on the last train she saw her reflection in the window like that, pale and pointed, looking sideways, fleering at the bugle eyes which were so very blot-like and black above cream-coloured cheeks. She had a vision of George coming up to her as she sat illegally alone in her accustomed first-class carriage, and saw his difficult smile.

Hugging herself as she rocked to and fro on the folding chair, adjusting her balance as it threatened to jack-knife her thighs to stomach in its fold-up maw, her hands became George's, firm and pressing around her waist. She stood up. Now one crept forward and undid the buttons of her shirt, stroked her neck down past the collar bone. Catching sight of herself in the mirror tweaking her own breast, the silly lost expression left her face instantly.

She reached across for Shakespeare and flicked through until she came to her latest discovery in *Antony and Cleopatra*. Holding her left hand palm out to her reflection, she touched wrist to wrist in the chill glass and murmured,

> There is gold and here
> My bluest veins to kiss, a hand that kings
> Have lipped, and trembled kissing.

This produced a reluctant simper and a slow shudder which wriggled through from head to foot finishing with a sigh. After a minute she tried it again but this time it did not work.

Lifting her knees and pointing her toes like a cartoon of stealth, she fell back onto her *As You Like It* essay with an angry groan.

> It was a lover and his lass,
> With a hey, and a ho, and a hey nonino
> That o'er the green corn field did pass
> In the spring time, the only pretty ring time
> When birds do sing, hey ding a ding ding.

'Anybody could write this sort of stuff,' she wrote. 'If Madonna put it in one of her lyrics, English teachers everywhere would say, how moronic.' Then she dashed off an inspired demolition job on Touchstone before losing her drift.

Flicking through the rice-paper leaves, she came to another juicy bit.

> Des: O, banish me, my lord, but kill me not!
> Oth: Down, strumpet!
> Des: Kill me tomorrow; let me live tonight!
> Oth: Nay, if you strive –

There was George, big George, looming like a tower in the half-dark, and herself in a white nightdress with pintucks from shoulder seam to waist, quite plain, no lace, his hot hands round her neck . . . She inhaled slowly and closed her eyes; leaned forward and pressed a bit against her windpipe with her thumbs; blushingly smirked; then felt a chill tinge of shame, a prickling under her arms like cactus hairs, and busily started to biro a blue swallow on the inside of her elbow.

Tattoos only lasted when the ink got into your bloodstream.

Maybe she would get her ears pierced this afternoon at Shangri La, she thought, though that was supposed to hurt a lot too, there was no anaesthetic, they just shot a spike through the lobe with a little gun like a paper punch.

She sniggered as she remembered something rude. According to Valerie Mitchell from 6B, who was a Saturday girl at Shangri La and who was doing Louis XIV for a special project, the Sun King's bed was heaped with pillows stuffed with his mistresses' hair. 'And not with the hair from their *heads*,' Valerie had leered.

Now she described this conversation to George in her make-believe letter, and even enclosed a clipping to launch his collection. When it came to signing off this time, she added fifty smacking Xs. She then spat on the paper before smearing it with her fist. Across the envelope's seal she wrote SWALK in lipstick and from the Queen's mouth on the stamp she drew a balloon saying, 'Who's a pretty boy then.'

'*Please* come and play,' whined her sister from the other side of the door. 'You've been up here for ages now and I don't believe you're just doing revision.'

'Go away,' she said.

'We could go roller skating,' said her sister.

'Mum won't let me go out till I've done the washing up,' she said, 'and I'm refusing on moral grounds since it's not my turn, so I *can't* go out.'

Once her sister had gone stump-stump-stumping off downstairs, she crept along the landing, pausing to stare and bite her thumb at the rumpled bedroom shared by her mother and stepfather. Then, when she was safely locked in the bathroom, she transferred all the plastic ducklings, sailors, mechanically spouting whales and dinghies from the bath to the lavatory and closed the lid on them.

During the chin-high soak which followed, she lay poaching in water so hot that a clear Plimsoll line appeared on her skin, all fiery lobster-coloured flesh below the water's surface while above stayed white and sweat-pearled. The little bathroom was dense with steam, the wallpaper's paisley invisible and the gloss-painted ceiling lustrous with moisture. She closed her eyes and saw George opening her letter, his crooked smile, his reaching for the telephone. They talked with sophisticated ease, and soon they were sharing a fondue down at the Mousetrap.

There was silence except for the rustle from the boa of weightless scented bubbles sitting on her shoulders. It came into her mind that it would be much more natural to give him a ring straight off, and she decided not to send the letter after all.

When at last she tottered back, lurid and wrinkled and dizzy, her sister was sitting on the bed.

'You've *got* to play with me now,' said her sister. 'I've done all your washing up and Mum says you're horrible but you can go out on condition you take me roller skating.'

'Shift up,' she croaked, collapsing onto the bed, clutching at disappearing shreds of George as the towels came adrift all round her.

'So you *will* come when you're dry,' said her sister, gnatlike. 'I've got your skates out. I've tidied your room, see, so Mum won't go on about that either. There's no excuse. I even went down the road to post your letters.'

'Letters,' she said stupidly, still stunned by the equatorial bath, before it dawned on her.

Let Nothing You Dismay

The tree was bigger than ever, eight feet tall, a bushy Douglas fir making the furniture round it look pathetically tame. Lametta icicles dangled from its needles, silver reflecting white from the snow outside, and little painted apples on ribbons. These apples transformed it into a medieval Paradise tree, absolved by Christ's birth from the curse laid upon it in the garden of Eden, though nobody in the house was aware of this, least of all fifteen-year-old Miranda Otway, who was lounging beneath its green boughs whispering sweet nothings down the telephone to Colin Smith.

A hard-faced boy came in, agitated the little snowscene of the man and woman standing in a forest, snapped off a sprig of mistletoe, and kissed Miranda, who covered the receiver and preserved a mouth of stone until he went away again. Then, 'Nothing,' she whispered. 'Just that creep Jasper I told you about that Daddy asked for Christmas.'

Over on the table by her father's armchair lay *The Pickwick Papers*, open at chapter twenty-eight in case any-

11

one should care to take up the flutter-leafed volume and read aloud in a plummy voice, as he, Tarquin Otway, paterfamilias, liked to do. The night before, on Christmas Eve, Tarquin had gathered them all round him to join in a rousing seasonal medley before supper, and there was his favourite volume of carols on top of the piano now, packed with opulent gallery-backed reproductions: a della Robbia virgin against blue-glazed heavens; Flemish magi; oak angels springing from carved choir stalls; seven satin-stitched swans a-swimming; a star sending golden streamers down to a gold-strawed crib.

'Do you know, the Deerhursts put a card through the door last night,' said Jane Otway, plucking her husband into the room by his shirtsleeve, pouncing on a glossy scene of gluttony above the fireplace. 'After we'd gone to bed. They are infuriating. They do it on purpose. They know we don't hit it off.'

'A cheap trick,' Tarquin agreed.

'I think Miranda has asked this new boyfriend to tea, by the way,' said Jane. 'So be warned.'

Miranda had meanwhile joined her five-year-old sister Susan in answering the door to their grandmother, and was now puzzling over twisted coatsleeve linings and spare cardigans.

'Happy Christmas, Mummy,' crowed Jane, coming into the hall. 'Happy Christmas.'

'If you say so,' said her mother, eyeing her narrowly. 'You're looking very fat, Jane. You're not pregnant again?'

'I can assure you she's not!' chuckled Tarquin, giving his mother-in-law a symbolic embrace, holding her for a moment as though she were a corn dolly or similarly fragile item of folk art. 'How are you, Cynthia?'

'Oh, you know,' she said, cross, flirtatious.

'A glass of ginger wine,' he announced in his glad ecclesiastical voice.

'I hate to think what's happening out there,' said Tarquin from the head of the table. 'She should have left it to me. I think I can safely claim to know more about geese than Jane does.'

'That wouldn't be difficult,' said Jane's mother, with a dry laugh.

'The inexperienced trying to cook the inappropriate,' said Tarquin. 'What was it Oscar said? The ignoramus, was it? The incoherent? Oh, something something something.'

Jasper chuckled sycophantically.

'Well, you'll be up at Oriel before we know it,' said Tarquin, turning to him fondly. 'You'll soon be able to put me right.'

'I can't eat this soup,' piped Susan. 'It's horrible.'

'*Soupe de poissons* from Marseille,' said Tarquin, 'is not horrible whatever else it is. I hope she's remembered to save the fat.'

'I can't eat the soup either,' said Miranda.

'Goose dripping sandwiches,' said Tarquin fondly. 'With a spot of vinegar. Oh, you. You can't eat anything. On principle.'

'Vegetarian!' said Jane's mother, and laughed.

'Vegetarian,' said Tarquin. 'Why can't you do something constructive. Like bell ringing. Gloria in excelsis. By

13

the way, where's this friend of yours "Colin" destined for?'

Miranda shrugged and stared at her plate.

'Oriel,' said Jasper thoughtfully. 'Only if my results are all right, of course.'

'They will be,' said Tarquin. 'Chip off the old block. Your father and I up at Oriel together. Squash, rugger, rowing, whatever you care to mention. Nights in the bar. Now I'm in Hertfordshire and he's in Melbourne. Extraordinary! Here's to Charlie, anyway. And we're glad to have you with us today, Jasper, as you couldn't join your own family.'

'Oh, plum pudding on the beach,' said Jasper. 'Not really my scene.'

'Anyway,' said Tarquin, raising his glass. 'To the family.'

'I don't know how you can, Daddy,' said Miranda. 'Pretending to be all nicey nice at Christmas when you hardly ever see us the rest of the year.'

'Somebody's got to pay your school fees, my dear,' said Tarquin with a tight smile. 'Put this not insubstantial roof over our heads.'

Just then, Jane tottered into the room on a cloud of steam like the genie of the lamp. When she had put the goose into the oven, three hours ago, it had been a large oval-breasted cadaver. During the morning she had had to pour off several pints of the fat which she now realized had been its chief constituent. Much of this fat seemed to have made its way onto her clothes and hair and skin. The goose, meanwhile, had continued to melt like a candle, and was

14

now rather less than half its former size. She placed it in front of Tarquin along with the carving implements.

'Another thing, Daddy,' Miranda was saying. 'We all heard you in church crackling that twenty-pound note before you put it on the plate. Talk about showing off.'

'Good will to all men,' said Tarquin pleasantly, shaving off fine-grained leaves of goose with expert relish. 'The time of year to think of those less fortunate than ourselves. Etcetera. You heard the vicar, Miranda.'

'Oh honestly,' said Miranda.

'Go on,' said Tarquin, tucking in. 'Tell me the homeless are all my fault. Beat me up with the cardboard boxes.'

'Twenty pounds,' said Miranda. 'It's an insult. You should give a tenth of your income. A third!'

'I already do, via the Inland Revenue. More!' said Tarquin. 'Now crush me with the single mothers.'

'The crib was a bit disappointing this year,' said Jane. 'Everybody thought so. The three kings were awfully drab. Anyway, Miranda, we've got a standing order with Save the Children.'

'Do you know what's happening in the world?' bellowed Miranda. 'Wars. Earthquakes. Torture. Then you pretend you believe in God.'

'I suppose this Colin is a lefty,' said Tarquin.

'Sometimes,' said Miranda, 'I really hate you.'

'Now, now, Tiny Tim,' said Tarquin. 'Or should it be Timette. Tiny Timette. Rather a good name for a large-boned girl like you. Should you choose to go in for prize wrestling.'

Jasper almost fell off his chair laughing.

Later that afternoon, Jane was preparing the tea.

'You will be nice to this Colin boy, darling?' she said to her husband, who was lolling against the kitchen dresser under a post-prandial cloud of alcohol.

'Some oversexed young yob brought home expressly to annoy me,' he grumbled, throwing a chunk of stollen into his mouth. 'To insult us.'

'You never know,' said Jane, fanning out a line of Dutch spice biscuits. 'He may be a very nice boy.'

And when at last Colin appeared, shifting from desert boot to desert boot on the doormat, it seemed that he was indeed exactly that. Tall, broad-shouldered, shy and beautiful, he was every inch the handsome prince. His long dark hair, spangled with six-cornered snowflakes, was tied back in a pony tail.

'Pleased to meet you,' he said, and with a horrified look watched himself wipe his hand on his trouser leg before offering it to Tarquin.

'Miranda will be down in a minute,' said Jane. 'Do come in.'

Colin loped over to the shelter of the sideboard, where he stood at bay, his eyes skittering over silver-coated almonds, muscatel raisins, and half a dozen Mandarin oranges, skinless, sodden, stacked in a crystal tower of Cointreau.

'We usually play a game or two before tea at Christmas,' said Tarquin. 'Do you like games, Colin?'

'What, er, you mean, cards?' said Colin.

'Well, I was thinking more of Botticelli,' purred Tarquin. 'Charades. That sort of thing.'

'Dumb Crambo,' said Jasper.

'Right,' said Colin. 'Right.'

There was a bowl of pot-pourri at his elbow, snuff-coloured rose petals, parched and faded; he grabbed a nervous handful, imagining them to be some sort of posh crisps, and thrust it into his mouth.

Everyone stared, transfixed, as Colin chewed. Susan said, 'Can I have one?'

Miranda came into the room, and her eyes met his. He gave an heroic swallow and gasped her name. They smiled at each other uncontrollably.

'How many brothers and sisters have you got?' piped Susan.

'Two brothers, both older than me,' he said, ruffling her hair. 'No sisters.'

'Oh,' said Susan, and stood hugging his left leg and smiling up at him like a kitten.

'I hope your mother doesn't mind us stealing you like this on Christmas Day,' said Jane.

'No,' said Colin. 'Mum died. Nearly three years ago now.'

'Oh I am sorry,' said Jane.

'Yeah,' said Colin. 'But we're all right.'

'Was it . . . ?' said Tarquin.

'Cancer,' said Colin.

'What, er, what sort?' asked Tarquin.

'Oh. Er. Lung cancer,' said Colin, lifting his chin.

'Ah.' Tarquin paused. 'She was a smoker, then?'

'Daddy!' said Miranda.

'Three years,' said Tarquin. 'Pretty much back to normal, I expect, now that the, er, dust has settled?'

'Not very cheerful at Christmas, though,' said Jane.

'It's not been that bad,' said Colin. 'My friend at school, now, he's had a bad Christmas all right. His mother ran off with her boyfriend in November, and his father, he's a drinker, he chucked him out last night. Nowhere to go. No money. He's dossing down with us for a few nights but my dad says he's got to be out by new year.'

'Where did you say you went to school?' said Tarquin. 'Near here? No, I thought not. So – er – how did you two meet?'

'That's enough, Daddy,' said Miranda. 'Come on, Colin. We need some air.'

Grabbing a duffel coat, she dragged Colin past the open-mouthed faces and ran off out of the house and into the snow, the branching shoots of melodrama sprouting enjoyably in her chest.

'Awful awful awful,' she sang, dancing ahead of him down the drive. 'I can't believe how awful they are. Escape!'

'Those crisps,' he said, shaking his head. 'Evil.' Then, 'Let's go.'

They ran together, puffing silver clouds into the icy air, down onto the main road, past the petrol station and over to the left along an overgrown lane leading to a track which took them up at last to the high fields. Here, the snow was untouched, its surface crust unbroken. They crunched to a halt at last, panting. The sun was low and red on the brow of the hill.

'They're all so crude,' she said, once her breath had come back. 'Going on at me about Aids and herpes all the time.'

'When I have children,' he began.

'I'm never going to,' she interrupted. 'They've put me off for good.'

'Don't say that,' he said.

He scooped up a fistful of the crumping snow and clasped her hands round it, then clapped his hands round hers. Inside, the snowball hardened, compacted down to the size of an egg. They stood and waited, and the ice water trickled out from between their knuckles and interlaced fingers.

'Not much left now,' she said.

He bent his head and kissed their coupled hands, then unfastened them. There was a small icy nugget the size of a squash ball. He took it and bit it and swallowed it down.

'There,' he said. 'I'd do anything for you.'

Their faces were pink as peonies, chilled on the surface but burning just beneath the skin. They stood hugging and kissing for a few minutes, warming their hands inside each other's coats, then Colin broke free and went tearing off into a series of high jumps and somersaults, shouting, leaping at the lowest branches of the oak trees and shaking off their moss of snow.

'Why are you doing that?' called Miranda.

'Why not?' he yelled. 'Come on!' This time he took her hand and ran with her to a new untrodden clearing.

They lay down side by side on their backs and scissored their arms up and down against the snow, their legs from side to side, laughing from deep inside their stomachs. When they stood up, there were two deep winged and robed indentations. They stared at each other with snow-dazzled eyes.

At this moment in the waning day something very

19

unusual happened. The cold air near the ground had been overlaid with a quilt of warmer air, and where the two airs kissed, so to speak, supersaturation occurred. This is quite a common event in the polar regions, though not in Hertfordshire, and Miranda and Colin stood astonished and entranced as castle-sized clouds of diamond dust floated down from the cloudless sky, a trillion ice crystals drifting and glittering in the light of the sun and the moon, to form halos, coronas, arabesques and other iridescent phenomena before their delighted gaze.

Then, very swift and silent, the last of the fabulous light trickled away. They started to shiver. Soaked in snowmelt, their wet clothes struck a chill beyond the flesh into their central bones. The dazzling crystalline pantomime had vanished into thin air, and they were left standing on a cold hill.

'Let's go,' said Colin.

They joined hands and started to run.

When at last they reached the street where Miranda lived, they stood outside the front door, doubled up and winded. Behind drawn curtains the rooms bloomed warm and domestic.

'Home and dry,' he panted.

'I don't want to go in.'

'Don't knock it. It's freezing out here.'

'But they really get me down.'

'You should feel sorry for them. They're stuck inside for good now.'

She flashed him a quick uncertain grin.

'Not like us,' he said, and they wrestled for a minute in a duffel-coated bearhug.

The front door opened onto the familiar hall with its holly-topped coat rack and ivy-wreathed telephone table, all bathed in yellow electric light.

'There you are,' said Jane in her dressing gown. Through another doorway they could see Susan, thumb in mouth, watching *Bedknobs and Broomsticks*.

'I was worried about you, darling,' said Jane.

'No need,' said Miranda.

'You're not feeling ill?'

'No. Why?'

'The fish soup,' said her mother sorrowfully. 'I thought it would be fine. Bottled in Marseille. Your father's been very ill. Both ends, I'm afraid. He's confined to the bathroom. And your grandmother was sick too, not so much, but they whisked her off to hospital overnight, just to be on the safe side. At her age. As for Jasper, he's had to forget that smart party he was going on to. He's not at all well. He's up in the spare room.'

'I'm all right,' said Susan. 'I didn't eat the stinky fish soup.'

'I missed it because I was dealing with the goose, of course,' said Jane. 'So I suppose I've got something to thank the wretched bird for. Even so, I've got a bit of a headache. It's all been a bit much. The fuss your father made! So now you're back I think I'll go to bed. See how he is.' She hitched up the hot water bottle she was carrying under her arm and wandered off towards the stairs.

'Good night,' they chorused.

Colin sat down between the two girls on the sofa and put an arm round each of them.

In front of them the television carried on regardless. A bed like a ship was speeding past mermaids and sea-horses, and its occupants were singing.

'Goody,' carolled Susan. 'Just us three.'

She turned to Colin pleadingly, and stroked his face.

'Can I do your hair in bunches?' she said.

The Gourmet

'Sometimes I can't stop,' she said, and threw a fistful of Japanese rice crackers into her maw with precise and startling violence. 'I can't control myself. Take them away from me!' She was giggling and crunching at the kitchen table, her back to the window, the last of the light turning her hair into a bonfire. Redheads have less hair to the scalp than the rest of us, but frequently they make up for this in coarseness.

'Is there anything you dislike?' I asked, knife poised, and she confessed to not being very keen on foreign muck. I almost yawned in her face at this bêtise, but she was exceptionally pretty so I controlled myself. Have you ever salivated wolfishly over some delicate noisette of milk-fed lamb? That was the variety of lip-smacking she provoked in me. She prattled on about her mum and her journey on the underground and how much dogs' mess there was on London's pavements while I watched her hotly from under my lizard lids.

Bending over her to pour a glass of wine I was relieved to find that she smelled only of herself and soap and water.

Taste is very largely smell, and many a promising meal has been ruined by Diorissimo.

'I'm sure you've heard of the seven deadly sins, Rosemary,' I said at random. 'But can you list the primary odours?'

Her eyes swivelled and frowned, and she swung them up sideways in ruminant pretence to the ceiling corner.

'Floral, putrid, pepperminty,' I rattled off, 'musky, pungent, ethereal, camphoraceous.'

The herb rosemary has a strong flavour of camphor, and I toyed with the idea of describing to her how spiritedly her namesake grows on the hillsides of the Luberon, or even, how a needle from its dried branches can be sharp enough to pierce the intestinal wall. But she was off again, telling me some story of mayhem in a pizza parlour, so I did not bother.

I placed a Venetian dish of risi e bisi in front of her, the Arborio rice fattened with peapod stock, the young peas sweet and fresh and infantine. She tucked in with an appetite.

Rice and peas?

Why not?

Let me explain now that the more traditional foods of seduction have always struck me as vulgar and unsuited to their purpose. What could be less aphrodisiac than to watch each other lipping the limp tips of flaccid though empurpled asparagus branches. I would always try to spare the blushes of a young person from such snigger-provoking simulacra as, cotechino, knackwurst, saucisses de Toulouse, or, God help us, ripe figs. As for the rehearsal for rape involved in serving oysters, it is something I find frankly embarrassing: the insertion and quick twist of the blade down at the clamped shell's hinge; slicing the bivalve's muscle from its bed; watching it flinch naked at the lemon juice; and at the last tossing it live down one's throat after a cursory gnashing to release flavour.

No, I restrict myself to verbal rather than visual puns, amusing myself without, I hope, alarming my guests.

'What's this?' asked Rosemary as I produced a platter of sizzled hammered veal slices overlaid with air-dried ham, each coupling fastened with a sage leaf and a toothpick.

'Saltimbocca,' I replied, baring my yellow teeth. 'Which, roughly translated, means, jump-into-the-mouth.'

'Yummy!' she chortled, and set to with a will. It did my old heart good to watch her, eyes bright, lips and teeth flashing with butter, deep in the act of mastication.

She was unused to talking during a meal, it seemed.

'We don't really eat together at home,' she remarked. 'We just help ourselves from the fridge when we get the munchies.'

I choose to cook for my young friends rather than take them to restaurants, not only to honour their youth and beauty but also to obviate the very real ravages of boredom. That stultifying chatter about personal fulfil-ment, the identikit aims and indignations, are ignorable as chaff if I can meanwhile be diverting myself in weaving a cage of hot caramel athwart the bowl of a ladle.

I gave her another plateful of saltimbocca, and she tucked in gratefully. Making the effort at last, I com-menced the real business of self-inveiglement, questioning her respectfully about her future career, listening with an appropriately impressed expression to her worries on behalf of the third world, and eventually posing gentle queries about her boyfriend situation. At this she started to sigh and wrinkle her forehead and even to sniff a little. I could hardly have been more tender towards her than she was towards herself. We nursed her little hurts, coddled the smarting, spoon-fed her self-esteem. I passed her a fresh damask napkin and she grinned and dabbed her eyes.

'That was *brilliant!*' she said as I cleared the plates. 'What was it again?'

Absently I listed the ingredients of saltimbocca, and it was at this point that she fell silent. To tell the truth I was not at all sorry at the cessation of her rather ugly suburban voice with its corncrake edge, stuffed to the gills with thanks-a-lots and ever-so-nices.

The kitchen was now in that strange domestic gloaming where steel and copper implements send out sharply unexpected gleams. I set assorted branches of candelabra in front of Rosemary and gave her a box of matches. In my experience, children like to play with fire, and she made the candles bloom like crocuses. Meanwhile I rolled little bundles of lollo rosso and peppery nasturtium leaves, then sliced them into a generous chiffonade.

I like to pay compliments to the individual beauties of my young guests in my choice of menu by introducing some subliminally referential food at a certain point in the meal. So it was that I had prepared sole bonne femme for stand-offish little Hannah and had baked piroshki for Natasha, wasted on her, of course, since she came from Tooting, but satisfying even so. For a certain toothsome Charlotte I had once assembled the eponymous Malakoff, equal parts of sugar, beurre d'Isigny, cream and ground almonds in a bucket-shaped mould lined with boudoir fingers. Now, for rufous Rosemary, I composed a salad punctuated with vivid orange nasturtium flowers to stand alongside the eccentric but indubitably orange cheese tray, upon whose plaited straw glowered a sunset wedge of Leicester, the same of Mimolette, a block of gjetost, ochreously fudge-like, and a very fair specimen of crumbling cadmium Cheshire. To complete this flush of rubicundity I opened a bottle of Chinon, softly purple.

'Do you like the wines of the Loire, Rosemary?' I asked.

Now that she had piped down, it was possible to concentrate on the neatness of her cat-like muzzle and the mournful set of her eyes, from which I could imagine creeping a pellucid tear or two. Despite my reassurances, she avoided nibbling the flowers, which denied me the frisson of marigold on vermeil. Never mind! She would have a greedy adolescent tooth for sweetness, I was sure, and so I prepared myself for the necromancy involved in concocting my chosen set piece, Iles Flottantes.

I scoured the copper bowl with a salted cut lemon until it winked pinkly, and while I did this I began to think less idly about the various conjunctions to be managed next door in the very near future. Bringing egg whites up to eight times their own volume with a balloon whisk is quite a little performance. The expressionless face, slight breathlessness and controlled energy of the rhythmically moving arm is nothing short of an erotic spectacle. I placed a folded towel beneath the bowl and commenced my exertions.

Rosemary stared. In her short life of boxed and tinned

meals she had probably never even seen an egg before, let alone witnessed what it can do.

A little later on in the proceedings, the poached drift of bubbled albumen floating in a shallow vanilla lake, myself crooning Purcell's *Fairest Isle* beneath my breath, I decided to crown all with a veil of malleable brittleness, and cast loose nets of spun sugar over the whiteness. While teasing out the thousand molten strands mid-air, I had been touched to catch my innocent imagination wandering off to a wedding breakfast in some wood, crimson fraises de bois heaped in an ice bowl set with wood anemones, all goatishness translated to the sound of Pan pipes in a glade of greening larch. An unwound scroll was pinned to the bark of a tree.

'Doubtless it reads, "The world must be peopled",' I scoffed to the Bard (off-stage).

Rosemary looked wise. I loved her silence. I led her to a low sofa, her docile little hand in my hairy paw, and she sank with the slight gasp they all make at its unexpected softness and lack of upright support. Then I made coffee and produced the illustrated matter which is my equivalent to after dinner mints.

In most cases they are so softened at being shown by my culinary efforts how much I *care* for them, so socially unsure of what's what, so intimidated by the whole process, that they automatically restrain any slight terror produced by the pictured suggestions. And during those faltering moments, of course, curiosity has time to sink its teeth in.

Not so with Rosemary.

'Oh yuk,' she said, and not merely her lip but the entire left side of her face appeared to curl.

I recoiled.

'It figures,' she sneered. 'I might have guessed. You're nothing but a dirty old man. I had a creepy feeling about you ever since you told me what was in that recipe. Pervert! Fancy tricking me into eating slices off some poor calf that's been hanging upside down with a slit neck, bleeding to death. It's made me sick to my stomach ever since.'

She carried on in this vein for some minutes while I wondered dismally how long it would take her to leave.

'I thought you were my *friend*,' she said. 'You were just *pretending*. I thought you really *liked* me.' She lapsed into trite whimperings of outrage. Then we had some more stuff about friends, and straight up, and on the level.

I considered informing her that she had been taken in by a trendy fib; that women and men are different and not *made* to be friends; that there is the consumer and the consumed; and so on. Her nastiness was escalating, however, and noise filled the room.

Some men prolong the moments before orgasm by remembering school dinners; similarly it is possible to divert tiresome and unproductive emotions by the cold arousal of disgust. I watched her closely as she ranted, noting the flecks of saliva flying into the candlelight, the half-concealed eructation half-way through the diatribe, and even, when I concentrated, the newly gathered fleece of plaque at the junction of her teeth and gums.

'Where's the toilet,' she demanded at last. Wordlessly I pointed, then listened for what seemed a very long while to a urination of equine copiousness and vigour. When she returned her nose was red and moist, her mouth as shapeless as a jellyfish. She couldn't leave fast enough for either of us.

I stood looking round me at the broken funeral baked meats. I had been deceived by the appearance of the fleshly envelope into believing its enclosure would be equally graceful. It wasn't her crudeness that had so disconcerted me, nor her easy sentimentality, nor yet the blinkered commonplaceness of her outlook. It was more that she now appeared to me in her true colours, as a camp follower to the Goths and Vandals, squatting down on her hunkers in the ruined courtyard of some library gnawing on a bone, belching out her contempt for civilization and *douceur de vivre*.

I felt saddened, and considered ringing the agency. But that dirty-minded girl had spoiled the impulse, she had muddied the crystal spring.

I twiddled a nasturtium flower. I drained a final atrabilious glass of Chinon. Then I carried what was left of my Floating Islands off to the refrigerator.

Bed and Breakfast

They sat side by side not holding hands. Back on the platform and in the ticket office, people had turned to stare at them. It was visible, the intensity of their candle power, joined, no matter how they tried to bank it down and look everydayish.

Proud and shy out in the public air, they avoided the larky or lovey-dovey behaviour common to their age group. It was enough to allow themselves to glance at each other now and then, glances arrowing beams of sheepish delight.

With a swish of doors and a sigh the train slid away. Light poured in through the smeary windows. Nicola lowered her eyelids and broke into a half-smile, the edges of her teeth showing in the sunny flood like a fringe of daisy petals. She was very fair. Simon looked sideways at her face, the snowy printless forehead, and then she, turning, opened her eyes straight into his and he blushed, gasped, burrowed in his sports bag and brought out a mathematically arranged cheese sandwich. This he placed furtively in her lap.

'To keep your strength up,' he muttered, frowning at the

couple opposite, fending off ridicule. The man was older than them, in his early twenties, stout, strong, sulky, his thumbs sunk angrily into the waistband of his jeans, muscular legs in a V-sign hogging more than their share of space. He was staring glumly out of the window as they sped past vegetable allotments and chimney stacks, his glare on autopilot. Beside him his girlfriend sat poring over a magazine article headed 'What Makes a Girl a Good Lay?'

These two ignored each other till the next station, when they slouched off the train like a couple of Alsatians. Nicola watched them snapping and snarling on the platform as the train pulled out.

'That's what we're *not* like,' she whispered, her lips like feathers against Paul's glowing ear-rim. 'We're not like that.'

'No!' he murmured, in frantic agreement.

All the talk of who fancied whom, who'd got off with whom, and words like shagging, she was above all that, he thought, it needed a quite different vocabulary to describe what was between them.

'Slag,' she'd said, for instance. 'If you ever use that word about anyone I'll never speak to you again. Or scrubber. Or dog.' He agreed with her, he was in no position not to. Half the time preoccupied, the *princesse lointaine*, miles away, and then the centre of attraction without even trying, you could feel the physical force of that phrase pulling power, she had it; though he should find a better way to put this, of course.

She had come into power certainly, but was, sweetly priggish, concerned not to abuse it. Daily she examined her emotions for signs of corruption.

Only last weekend she had told him about the two German students who had followed her round Boots, who'd kept asking her out, quite politely, and when finally she had said, no, really no, they had left meekly, one of them pausing first to say, 'Thank God indeed that he has made such beautiful faces for us to look at.'

'Bastard,' Simon had said before he could help it. Then, after a gratified smirk, she had looked embarrassed and even apologized.

The three other passengers in their carriage were all disembarking. Nicola and Simon looked at each other and waited, taut, until the doors sighed unevenly and they were quite out of the station, then collected themselves into each other's arms with a mutual groan. Their eyes flickered shut, their lips pressed open each to the other's, she curved her hand round his bare neck while he twisted his fingers in her hair during the unstoppered kisses. His hand moved to cover her breast, she smudged her heated face into his hot neck with a sigh, and his body pressed trembling, heavy and graceful against hers.

This was nothing to do with anybody else, and was certainly light years from those distant shameful sessions in the Bio Lab with the video and the Tupperware lunchbox full of contraceptives. There had been a pungent smell coming from the earthworms slit lengthwise in half and staked out with dressmaking pins half an hour earlier by the first year. À propos of nothing they had been plonked in front of the mooing woman, so hefty, so gross compared with the wildflower girls whom the documentary had devastated in front of the boys. Then the stirruped splay and bloody debouchment, to which the pious voiceover had instructed them to respond with wonder, with awe, had made even the snickering boys go green.

'They weren't being educational there, that was just propaganda,' she'd fumed. 'That was meant as a deterrent. How dare they.' Therefore she had rejected the whole lot, the official sentimental education on offer, part and parcel, and was determined to reinvent the business of love for herself. Her attitude was the determined opposite of pragmatic. It took some nerve. She was the Lydia Languish of her set.

At the next station a flurry of new people piled in. This time the two of them sat opposite each other, looking out of the windows, turning occasionally for another secretive dazzled exchange of eyes. They rested their heads against carriage seats upholstered in shabby prickling green stuff which lit up under the sun like moss. They had never been properly alone together before, they were too young, they were both still living at home. They could not bear the thought of any of their various parents or step-parents or siblings knowing, so they had met in parks or walked by railway tracks, but it was the end of summer now and it was driving them mad.

They wanted something but weren't quite sure what they wanted. It was to do with something vital, though, it was there at the centre of their nascent sense of selfhood, and it was this which had caused to spring up the fierce protective hedge of silence and pride around the one area of their lives where they perceived their elders had no business, nor anybody else either.

'It's got to be *right*,' Nicola insisted.

'What will make it right?' asked Simon.

'We'll just know,' she said, confident, Rousseauesque.

It was difficult to convince her it was right when they could never be alone in a room together. Simon shared a room with two brothers, Nicola shared with her sister, their homes were packed to the gills and the fastidious simply did not thrive.

'I don't feel I belong to myself properly yet,' she had told him a while back. 'Dad's always on about how much I'm costing. I don't feel I'm my own property, not my body anyway. He does it sometimes to the plate of food in front of me, tots up how much the chips cost, the pie, the beans.'

That was why they were on this journey. Simon had found a guide in the library and chosen a place for the sake of its rural name, Meadowsweet, and, though he had not mentioned this, because it was the cheapest; although even so it was not cheap by the standards of what they could afford, in fact quite the opposite.

She leaned over and touched his arm. It was their station. All at once, there they were, deep in the country, standing on a tiny platform in the startlingly clean sweet air. Once the train had gone it was very quiet. They both jumped at a scuttering noise, but it was only a dry leaf bowling along the tarmac. Then they embraced, swaying, until they were light-headed, giddy, drawing away from each other with enormous smiles, almost shyly.

Simon got his map out.

'I think it might be quite a way,' he said, starting to look worried. 'There don't seem to be any buses either. Or taxis.'

'Oh, taxis,' said Nicola, as if she were sick to death of taxis. 'You don't go to the country for taxis. You *walk* in the country.'

35

They examined the map together, and it could have meant anything since it was the first time either of them had tried to use one.

'Let's see where that leads,' he said, pointing to a green lane edged with hawthorn bushes, for no other reason than that he liked the look of it.

The first five miles or so were in daylight, or at least, dusk. They followed the single track road past flat tilting fields and hedgerows with little brown birds jumping in and out of them. A mistiness and moistness of rain in the air pressed coolness to their faces and blurred their hair with droplets. As they walked, they discussed life, death, and later on, when it became relevant, the weather.

Their voices piped away into the evening.

'Truth,' said Nicola.

'Not using other people,' they agreed solemnly.

'Love,' said Simon. 'Who you love.'

They stopped to hug each other. He squeezed her so hard that her breath came puffing out, her ribs creaked and her feet left the ground.

'I feel incredibly strong,' he marvelled. 'I feel I could lift you to the top of that tree with one hand.'

They compared notes on how, in each other's company, they felt full of power, flickering like flames, capable of tremendous effortless speed; and how this fading light was lovely and mysterious, seemingly criss-crossed with satiny threads of excitement. They made each other feel so alive, they agreed; all those other people on the train, they'd been dozy, half conscious in comparison.

She picked a blade of grass, stretched it between her

thumbs and pursed her lips to blow. Kid's stuff, he pronounced this, copying her, and soon their piercing whistles split the air for half a mile around.

Time passed. It grew dark. The sky was a black meadow of silvered *petits moutons*; a gibbous moon backlit the scalloped border of each cloudlet. Some five or six fields away they could see a pub, a far-off gaudy box of rhythmic noise.

'We could ask there,' said Nicola.

'Too far,' said Simon. He peered at the map. 'Soon we hit a B-road, then we're laughing.'

'Can I have a look?' said Nicola. 'Ah. Mmm. I think we're here, look, that last church was marked. And, I see, that's where we're going. Yes. Quite a bit further.'

It started to rain.

By the time they reached the Meadowsweet Guest House it was nearly ten o'clock. They were drenched. Simon pressed the doorbell, and flashed her a desperate grin, like a plague victim. She returned a distant smile.

'We've got those chimes at home,' she said pensively. 'I didn't think they'd have them in the country.'

The door opened a crack and a suspicious bespectacled face peered at them over the guard-chain. Simon stepped forward.

'We booked,' he said. 'Simon Morrison.'

'It's ten o'clock,' said the face.

'It was a bit of a way from the station,' said Simon.

'You *walked*?' said the face disbelievingly. There was the scrabble and clink of various security measures being unfettered, then they were in, wiping their feet like a couple of children in the narrow hall.

'And you are Mr Morrison?' said their host, staring at Simon, who was looking his most half-baked.

'Thass right,' murmured Simon.

Their host's wife came to stare.

'I don't know,' she said at last. 'Come on, leave your wet shoes on the mat, then I'll bring you both a hot drink in the lounge.' She shook her head and bustled off, tutting, to the kitchen.

In the lounge, the leaping screen of the television was just one brightness among many. The room was small and savagely lit by a 150-watt bulb refracted through a complex chandelier which tinkled madly as Simon's head brushed it.

'Derek and Janet, I'd like you to meet our two strangers in the night,' said their host, who had decided to revert to jollity. 'Simon and, er.'

'Nicola,' said Nicola grimly. She and Simon stood awkwardly, sodden, in their socks. She glanced at him. He looked as though he wanted to hide behind the curtains. He looked, she thought, like a big child.

Derek and Janet gaped up at them from the settee.

'Raining, is it?' said Derek at last, gazing at Nicola's dripping elf-locks and rats-tails.

'Just a bit,' laughed their host, rubbing his hands. 'She looks like a little mermaid, doesn't she.' He put his arm matily round her shoulders. 'Sit ye down, Nicola, sit ye down.'

'Hot chocolate,' said his wife coldly from the door.

Up in their room at last, Nicola fell like a stone onto one of the twin beds.

'At least it's warm,' volunteered Simon. 'Clean. We can push the beds together.'

'No we can't,' snapped Nicola. 'I'd rather be under a haystack. This isn't the country. It's just like back at home.'

'It's the country outside, though,' said Simon, trying to draw her to him.

She shrugged him off.

'Nylon sheets,' she said bitterly. 'Horrible butterflies all over the duvet covers. Horrible little ornaments, rabbits in crinolines, mice on penny farthings.'

'But that sort of thing,' he said, amazed, 'it doesn't matter. I hadn't even noticed.'

'No, well,' she said. 'I thought, I thought at least there would be cotton sheets.'

'But that doesn't *matter*,' he persisted, earnest and gawky beneath another searchlight. 'Not at all. That's nothing.'

'Oh is it,' she sniffed.

'It sounded OK in the guide,' he said. ' "Cosy and welcoming". We couldn't afford the ones with stars.'

'Don't,' she said, turning away from his boy's face. The caparisoned fairytale personage had reverted to plain lizard.

'You'd like me more if I was five years older. Ten. And my skin puts you off,' he said. 'Be honest.'

'Shut up,' she said, and started to cry. He sat down beside her and tried to draw her into his shoulder. She resisted. He swore. She cried harder.

'Please Nicola,' he said, pacing the room. 'It can't be just the duvet covers.'

39

'It's not!' she said wildly. 'It's life!'

'How do you mean?' he said. 'Life.'

'Look,' she snarled, 'can't you see it ahead? We're going to end up like them.'

'Never,' he soothed.

'Boring. Dead!'

She was restlessly beating her foot. A violent cyclonic mood would arrive like this sometimes, inexplicable, devastating, tearing through one or the other of them like a runaway freight train leaving maximum damage in its wake. She shuddered.

'Can't you see?' she said, trying to be calm. 'We'd struggle along for a bit but we'd never get beyond this. It's all mapped out.'

He held his arms out to her, trying to hug her, but she cackled like a witch and shrank away.

'All those feelings of flame,' she continued, 'speed, being strong, they're rubbish, you know. They're just like the adverts, rubbish to keep us quiet for a bit.'

'Not what I feel for you,' he said stubbornly. 'That's real.'

'No,' she said. She was hurtling downwards now, nothing could stop her. 'Like my dad says, it's shaft or be shafted.' She thumped the bouncy foam pillows. 'Like he says, what makes me think *I'm* so special?'

'You are,' he said.

'Not long before I'm screaming at some man in front of the children, just like Mum. *If* he's still there.'

'I'd never leave you,' he said sadly.

'You say that now,' she scoffed.

And so they continued under the comfortless white glare, for several hours, until they fell asleep at last athwart the winsome bed linen, fully dressed, clasped in each other's arms, as dawn broke over the fields outside their bedroom window.

Summoned to breakfast by a peremptory knock at the door and a brusque Wakeywakey! from their host, they shuffled downstairs white-faced and red-eyed. The morning sun winked on stainless steel toast racks and tea in tin pots, it put a shine on the varnished sausages, and cruelly exposed the pallor of bacon fat, the bluish jelly on fried eggs.

Nicola sat glowering at the pink-jacketed hunting melée on her table mat, ignoring everything and everybody around her. Even so, Simon was not cowed. An hour ago he had had an amazing dream, a tremendous panoply of sensualism, intensely gratifying, shudderingly happy, easy. It had unfurled a prospect of utmost melting pleasure, and she was in it all right, right at the heart of it. He felt full of optimism. He wanted to tell her, she looked so gloomy, but decided it could wait.

The room was cramped, and the two other couples at neighbouring tables were whispering like embarrassed children, although they were in late middle age. The clatter of cutlery was deafening in this tense demi-silence.

'Soft-boiled I think you said, Peter,' sang their host, re-entering the room with the air of a man under extreme pressure. 'And fried for you, Marjorie. Now have I got that right.'

'You're not from these parts originally?' chirruped Marjorie, cocking her head up at him, brave in the hushed room.

'No, no,' smiled their host. 'Does it show? We've only

recently moved from Berkshire. Hence the tablemats. And you?'

'We're from Norfolk,' said Marjorie. 'Originally.'

'Ah, from Norfolk are you. The land of the lazy wind – it doesn't go round you, it goes through you.'

'That's right!' said Marjorie gaily, as though this were a fresh thought to her, a surprise.

'Now, can I tempt you to another sausage, Marjorie?' said their host, courtly in his offer. 'There's one going begging here.'

'No really, I couldn't,' protested Marjorie. 'I've had sufficient.'

'Oh come now,' said their host roguishly. 'Haven't you got a little crack? A leetle leetle crack? I think you have!'

Simon was grabbed by a terrible rude desire to laugh. He frowned and coughed, but low down inside him it was taking over. He glanced at Nicola's stony face and away again quickly.

'Just one weeny sausage!' wheedled their host. 'Go on, Marjorie. I'm going to be very upset if you can't fit it in, very disappointed.'

With an imploring pout he waved his offering temptingly beneath her nose.

'Just for me!' he leered.

Simon's eyes started to stream. His face disintegrated and rapidly he took cover behind his napkin. He began to whimper softly, trying to disguise it with coughing. Now Nicola too unwillingly succumbed. Shoulders heaving, she looked at him, alarmed, her breath starting to come in uneven shudders. Hastily, they stumbled up from their table, appalled, jostling each other like cattle in their hurry to get through the doorway, then clattered up the stairs, almost out of control.

The door of their room closed safe behind them, they fell onto their beds, sobbed into the pillows, they hooted until their ribs hurt and they had to hold their sides. Whenever either of them showed signs of calming down, the other caught their eye and they were off again.

'Oh don't,' they groaned. 'No more.'

The gloomy shreds of the hateful night they had passed in that room flapped off into the hinterland on leathery broken wings. They paid and left as soon as they were able.

Outside it was a morning of hot sun with a cool surfy breeze, the air like clear liquid with bubbles rising, and they gulped great effervescent draughts as though newly escaped from prison.

Everything around them looked beautiful or interesting, freshly oxygenated as they were to the point of euphoria. Weeds, long and lush but on their last legs, fringed the lane, and they saw that the greenish-white flowers of the stinging nettles were giving way to tassels of seeds. Blackberries in the hedge were still pale pink or purplish, underjuiced, too sour to eat yet. They spat out sample mouthfuls.

Simon dethorned a branch of early rosehips, light orange, large and impeccably lacquered, broke off the top three inches, heavily fruited, and stuck it behind his ear. Considering what a disaster last night had been, he felt surprisingly jubilant, almost as though they had triumphed over circumstance after all. That was because he felt sure that nothing important was stopping them from doing so. In fact, he realized, he was quite certain that it would be all right now. His dream warmed him, a smug heap of gold in some inward chamber of his mind. He smiled fatly, scooped Nicola up and swung her round in the air, ululating.

Having missed their breakfast earlier, they bought bread and cheese at the next village, silent while the elderly woman who was serving them chatted on to her crony about somebody else's unacceptable behaviour, cuddling the cordless phone between her chin and shoulder as she sliced the half-pound of cheddar.

Most of the cottages they passed had gardens visible from the road, all given over to vegetables. They paused to stare at a row of tall green teepees stuck with scarlet flowers.

'They're for cucumbers, aren't they?' said Simon uncertainly.

'I don't know,' said Nicola. 'But those over there are cabbages. Definitely. And that's rhubarb! I could grow rhubarb if I lived in the country.'

'Rhubarb?' said Simon, startled.

'Not *just* rhubarb,' she said, embarrassed. 'But, think, if you were vegetarian round here you'd need hardly any money.'

A few steps on by the side of the road was a carrier bag full of apples, in front of it a handwritten sign saying HELP YOURSELF.

'Look at that!' said Simon, amazed. He walked all round the bag as though some trick must be involved.

'You see?' said Nicola, choosing a couple of unbruised

apples. 'You wouldn't need much money living out here. You could keep hens too. Bees, even.'

'I don't know about bees,' frowned Simon. 'You have to know about these things.'

As they walked on, they marvelled at how nobody in the country seemed much under sixty, and doubted they would ever be able to afford somewhere to live. They touched on the captiousness of their parents, the advantages of tents and caravans, and wondered whether or not common land really was common these days. They talked about who owned what, and how, and why, and contemplated the traveller's life, the blessed freedom, the openness to weather, even bad weather, and the fate of travellers who fell ill or grew old. Nicola put forward the view that it would have been preferable to live in the old days, at least you could put up a fight then, they'd got everybody taped now; Simon disagreed, pointing out that she would have been blackleading the grates up at the big house until carried off by TB or the umpteenth baby, they were better off now, more able to live free even if it seemed otherwise sometimes, and he had faith, things would change.

On they walked, past fields just harvested, the stubble in burnished zigzags against the earth, bales of hay stacked like great slabs of golden cake.

'This is what I wanted,' said Nicola, pausing at a gate and flinging out her arms towards the fields, the cool bright air, golds and ochres turning miles away to bluish greys and greens, and on, rising up to the sky, a fierce tender blue, and cohorts of cumulus clouds, banked and ranked as far as the eye could see, luminous, their top curves taking the sun.

They climbed over the gate and threw down their jackets under a tree in the corner of this field with a view. Here they spread their picnic and hungrily made up for their earlier frustrated breakfast.

'Last night,' she said as they finished eating, and she flushed a sudden miserable red. 'I didn't. I mean, I wasn't. I felt so, you know. I thought I could *kill* myself.'

'Don't,' he said. 'It's gone. But this morning . . . That business with the . . . "There's one going begging!" '

He started to gasp again, looking at her in momentary surprise.

' "Go on, Marjorie," ' she remembered, joining him. 'Oh her face!'

The irresistible joke had come to life again, helium-filled. They fell on their backs and abandoned themselves to it, it was like some drug, the laughing, leaving a wake of foamy euphoria.

When they calmed down at last they were lying side by side, quite private, looking at the leafy canopy above them from whose shelter issued the thoughtful soothings of wood-pigeons. They turned and lay in a sideways hug, staring into each other's eyes, smiling occasionally.

'Last night,' murmured Simon after a while. 'Last night wasn't so bad after all.'

He nuzzled up under her chin and blew softly into her hair, into her neck, to foment his nerve. Then, although no one else was anywhere in sight, let alone hearing distance, he began to whisper his dream into her ear.

When in Rome

They were standing in front of the bronze Etruscan she-wolf, staring at her eight pendant dugs and the two hearty Roman babies suckling there. It was quite early, but the July heat had collared them, limp as they already were after a broken night of what Geraldine was starting to call hate-making.

'Romulus and Remus,' read Paul from his guide book. 'Twin sons of Mars, set adrift in a basket on the Tiber, rescued and raised by a she-wolf. Later Romulus killed Remus and established the city of Rome on the Palatine Hill.'

'Let's move on,' said Geraldine. 'I want to see the Caravaggio.' She took her hair in one hand and gave it a sharp twist so that it stayed up for a few moments, a thick and fairish tangle, baring her neck. She had Germanic colouring but was now patchily brown-faced, with light eyes thrown into bizarre holiday relief like pieces of turquoise mosaic. Paul was as dark as a Roman to start with, and the sun had seeped into his skin like ink into blotting paper.

'Romulus's new city was exclusively male,' he continued. 'So to remedy this sorry state of affairs the first
Romans kidnapped and raped the women of the neighbouring Sabine tribe.'

'Sorry state of affairs,' snorted Geraldine. 'Honestly.'
Her hair tumbled down in slow motion like a pile of
weeds.

They were stuck in an ageing deadlock, moody, critical,
not sure how to leave each other or whether to carry on.
Soon, they knew, the time would come to slough off
lifelessness and stand apart in fully fledged separate fury.
Meanwhile, since their arrival in Rome he had started
flirting with a new idea in a dangerous last-ditch sort of
way, and she had colluded to some extent. At any rate she
had grown rather careless; not being happy made her
childish. She buried the nagging thought alive.

'Strange to think *they* could do that,' said Paul, brushing
his knuckles across her breasts.

'What?' she said, looking at the she-wolf. 'Oh. Ah.'

Outside in the Forum the heat was almost African. At
first they tried to make sense of the bases of walls, the
stumps of former colonnades.

'Remains of the Basilica Julia,' read Geraldine. 'A court
of Civil Law. Forum of Augustus. The Mamertine Prison.'

Arches and columns and basilica fragments stood
around them like meaningless mountains.

'Next on the list,' he said, taking the book from her. 'The
Colosseum. Seated fifty-five thousand. Several hun-
dredweight of sawdust was spread over the ring between
each spectacle to absorb the blood.'

'Let's give it a miss,' she said.

'Don't move,' said Paul, pointing his camera at her. 'No, don't squint like that. Come on, Geraldine! You're on holiday, remember.'

She held still for some moments then lost patience and made an irritable movement just as he clicked the shutter. It was always like this when he was taking a photograph, she fumed to herself, the fatal lack of timing. Then the prints would come back with her face in a blur, or blinking, or glaring out with orange eyes like wasps.

'The sheer scale of it,' he said. He was polished with sweat, his skin like smooth dark marble.

'It's *too* big,' she sighed.

'It *was* the centre of the world,' he reproved.

Oh, we've got to talk on like this, ping, pong, for days and days yet, she thought. She turned her head restlessly, taking in the sepia-coloured landscape.

'The trouble was, of course, it went on too long,' he mused. 'The Roman empire. In the end it just crumbled.'

'Goths and Vandals,' she responded politely. 'Let's find an ice cream.'

By the time they reached the hotel for a siesta, the heat was stupendous. They had walked doggedly back in the sultry grey haze along packed roads buzzing with Vespas and helmetless boys and girls. Geraldine saw a man lean back at the traffic lights and kiss the girl sitting pillion, over his shoulder, almost upside down, top lip to bottom lip at any rate.

'All those obelisks and elephants,' she gasped, taking in their dim room, the *due letti* with narrow springless mattresses like squashed sandwiches, damp and white.

'You forget how close it is to Egypt,' Paul agreed.

'Carthage. The Phoenicians.' He stripped his clothes off and stood quietly in the shuttered gloom.

'You look like a statue,' she said.

She went and stood beside him, skated her fingertips idly over his damp torso. Their mouths smudged sideways into each other and she closed her eyes, started to lean into him and not think until, like a bee stinging, he bit the inside of her lip with a shade more spite than enthusiasm.

'Ouch,' she said, drawing back. 'I think I'll have a shower.'

'No,' he drawled, 'not yet,' and reeled her into him like a fisherman.

They cooled off each other for days at a time, then came together like this, almost in combat, gladiatorial. They turned cruel little blades on each other and wreaked havoc, and sulked; then made it up with a practised weariness – or in a fit of unpleasant excitement. This heat which so doped the mind did not similarly inhibit the body. They moved in on each other ferociously, both growing hotter by the second, so that it seemed for some blind free seconds that it was not sweat in which their bodies were slithering and slapping, but blood.

Afterwards they slept, and woke, sad, self-contained, and solicitous towards each other. Either it was like that now, or it was pointless and petered out. He approached her body with boredom, really, if he was honest, pressing buttons as if he were entering his PIN number in the cash machine, the familiar formula. And she, she turned her head to one side, eyes scrolling back, and thought, 'If he does that once more . . .'

That evening they ate their meal under a wooden pergola twisted with vine leaves. The day's quilt of heat had not lifted and it was still suffocatingly hot and soupy. A storm was working itself up. They sat pushing scraps of squid round their plates, and their talk was quite dead.

'Oh,' said Geraldine. 'Oh . . . it's so . . .'

She was plagued by vanished words; what they used to affirm over meals on past holidays had sounded then in her ears with operatic courage and significance. The trouble was, she couldn't now remember what it was that had been said. She half rose from the table, sighing, staring at him.

'What is it?' he asked coldly.

She subsided. Her hands moved nervously, fingers raking her hair back, then arachnid, rolling bread pellets. He disliked intensely these fidgety hands, also the self-pitying twist of her mouth and the squawky shrillness that shredded her voice when she grew agitated. She glared at his shut face, and huffed and puffed, feeling his bulk across the table as if it were some piece of meaningless masonry she would have to drag along with her forever, uphill.

'It's this place,' she said wildly. 'Rome. It's so oppressive! All the hugeness and efficiency. Cruelty.'

'You mean ancient Rome,' he corrected her. 'There's nothing very efficient about it now. No hot water at our hotel for two days. Those Americans are going crazy.'

'You always,' said Geraldine, and stopped.

'I always what?'

'Nothing.'

'No, come on,' said Paul. 'What?'

'On and on,' moaned Geraldine. 'Relentless.'

'In what way precisely,' said Paul.

'Inexorable!'

'First Rome,' he said. 'Now me.'

'What I mean is,' she shrilled, and he wished he could pick up that napkin and roll it into a ball and stuff it into her mouth. 'What I mean is, ancient Rome, it was all so bloody pragmatic. Baths and bridges and brothels and feasts and a special room to make yourself sick so you could go back and stuff more down your gullet. The vomitorium.'

'The vomitorium wasn't for vomiting in,' he said, scornful, pedantic. 'It was a particular sort of exit. From the Colosseum, actually, I think.'

'Shut up,' she shrilled. 'All I know is, there's more to life . . .'

'Oh yes, than the boring practical details,' he said nastily. 'Leave them to other people. Lesser mortals. Insurance and punctuality and all that. You're on the side of the Etruscans, aren't you, the shifty little singing dancing Etruscans with their sneaky little smiles.'

There was a silence, broken at last by a nervous bubbling giggle from Geraldine.

'You do hate me, don't you,' she smiled.

'Not at all, not at all,' he frowned – he was almost shouting now – 'But you're such a – such a dilettante, darling. Honestly.'

'How do you mean?' she asked, bridling, aware of the half-clothed affront waiting in the wings. He smiled.

'What I mean, Geraldine, what I mean is, all your talk of loving life, being happy just to be alive and so forth, as opposed to me, black and rigid and all that, well, it's just not on, is it. Life! You refuse to engage seriously with life at any level.'

They waited for the bill in silence, savouring the preceding exchange with a sort of scab-picking decadent relish; then walked slowly on to the Piazza Navona.

'I like the palm tree,' said Geraldine, as they walked around Bernini's Fontane dei Fumi. 'That must be the Nile. There's the Ganges, and see, on this corner is the Danube, and this last one's the Rio de la Plata. Look here, Paul, I don't want to settle down. Stay in.'

'That's just shallow talk,' said Paul. 'You can't know that.'

Lightning cracked the sky for an instant, a white flash, and then the rain came down in big warm splashy drops.

'Ah,' said Geraldine, 'I can't bear you,' and climbed into the floodlit fountain. The pale green water lapped round her legs, the rivergods lolled above in muscular abandon, and she stood in the drench, laughing, her streaming hair in long black rats-tails.

'For pity's sake,' said Paul in disgust. He turned on his heel and walked to the doorway of S. Agnese in Agone for shelter, and to disassociate himself from this display. A couple of Italian teenagers hooted and shouted before joining her in the water, and soon after that some American college girls jumped in and started singing 'I hear thunder'. This was what he couldn't stand about her, he muttered, as the rain drummed down so thickly that the fountain became a blur; this awful factitious edge. This hysteria.

The storm continued without any loss of energy, and a

little while later the fountain dancers climbed out and shook themselves and embraced with laughter and yelling before running off for shelter. Geraldine started off in the direction of the hotel, and he had to run to catch her up.

'I thought you'd grown out of all that,' he shouted as they jogged on side by side.

'All what?' she said, not looking at him.

'That wild woman of the woods act,' he said grimly.

'You hate me,' she panted.

'I bought you those shoes,' he said, and his voice was peevish. 'They're ruined.'

'That does it,' she said. 'I must have been mad. For the rest of this holiday, I'm serious, I *won't*, unless you get some things.'

'What?'

'Look, Paul. You know exactly what I mean. You encouraged me to be careless. But I'm not risking it. It's not flirting any more. I can feel people want it, you do anyway, as a sort of revenge. You don't want me swanning around. So if you want to . . .'

He did, actually, want to, very much, annoyingly enough; he wanted her underneath him and crying. He felt furious. He stopped and yanked her head back, tugging on a handful of hair, pushing his mouth on hers so that their teeth clashed together. When she tried to wriggle off he stuck his thigh between her legs.

'All right,' she hissed when he let go at last. 'But I mean it.' She ran off in the rain towards the hotel, while he tracked down an all-night chemist.

Afterwards they lay exhausted, having battled their way to a weary state of truce, slogging it out like veterans.

'This is getting monotonous,' whispered Geraldine, stroking his arm. He teetered on the verge of sleep, then pushed himself to get up and go to the bathroom. Once there, he saw what had happened, and woke up.

'Bloody Catholic condoms,' he muttered. He washed and went back slowly to the bedroom. Crouching beside her on the bed, he put an ear down close to her belly.

'What are you doing?' she asked sleepily.

'Listening,' he said. 'I can hear a sort of ticking noise under the gurgles. But maybe it's just your watch.' He gave a guilty laugh. 'You'll never guess what just happened.'

'You wouldn't think of doing anything about it, would you,' he murmured, nuzzling her ear, turning his face into her hair.

They were lounging in the afternoon sun on the curving Spanish Steps, one among scores of couples, clasped in a baroque embrace.

'That would be my business,' she whispered, pulling his face down into her neck.

'Not really,' he said, smudging the words into her breastbone. 'Not any more.'

'Listen, Paul,' she said, pulling away a little and kissing his eyelids. 'That's between me and my maker.'

Earlier that day they had visited the Vatican, and Geraldine had lain supine on a vacant stretch of marble in the Sistine Chapel in order to stare up for an unblinking minute at the creation of Adam, whose portrait was so astonishingly full of grace and power, half-rising to touch forefingers with God, so heart-stopping in its masculine beauty, that she had given an involuntary moan of pain when she saw, just beyond, the lumpish figure of Eve climbing from sleeping Adam's side as clumsily as if from a low slung sports car.

'It would be nothing but good for you,' he whispered, his arm over her shoulder and his lips brushing her earlobe, just like an Italian. 'You're not really rooted at the moment. You've said so yourself. Too light.' He punctuated these words with clever little kisses, beneath her eyebrow, by the corner of her eye, at the border of her upper lip. She gave a quivery laugh.

'It would be a sort of paperweight, you mean,' she suggested, butting her breasts against his ribs with a series of little sighs. He kissed her on the mouth, and they sat and rocked like this, locked, for a long time, as luxuriously tender as any couple there.

A little later, in Babington's Tea Rooms, they sat, hands linked across the tablecloth as though in farewell, and worked out that they were both almost ten years older than Keats had been when he died. At the table to their left were two palely glistening English couples of about their own age. These husbands and wives were giving each other long detailed descriptions of meals consumed, hoteliers' shortcomings, children's schools, own schools, and from there, amazing coincidences, greeted with faint screeches of delight.

'Johnny Pitlow? You know Johnny Pitlow? But that's incredible, he's godfather to my best friend's little girl, you know, the one who's at Lapwing House.'

'I simply could not, Paul,' whispered Geraldine in the

silence which had thickened between them. 'I couldn't do it, you know.'

'It doesn't have to be like that,' he said testily.

'But don't you see?' she hissed. 'We've only got each other to take care of and we can't even manage that.'

'Rubbish,' he said.

'Look at Kate,' said Geraldine urgently. 'All that awful juggling and fretting she went through, about maternity leave and all the rest of it. Then Nick walked out, and you said, the last time we saw her, you weren't surprised, she'd grown so morose, what's the matter with her, it's healthy isn't it, she looks as old as the hills, she should pull herself together.'

'You'd manage it better,' said Paul, wincing as he chewed on cinnamon toast. 'I think I'm getting a mouth ulcer,' he added thoughtfully, probing the lining of his cheek with his tongue.

'Poor Kate,' sighed Geraldine. 'I must send her a postcard.'

Out in the heat, they smiled with relief to be among beautiful Romans again. The passeggiata had started in the via del Corso, and they strolled along in synch, thigh spliced to thigh, aware that they were considerably longer in the tooth than their Italian counterparts.

'You look so lovely,' said Paul, stopping in the middle of the street to frame her face with his hands. 'It's a pity you're so selfish.'

'Selfish?' said Geraldine, latching on to that word. 'I only want to stay as I am.'

'Exactly,' said Paul, and his mouth folded into a censorious line. He walked on alone.

'What's selfish about that?' said Geraldine, running after him.

'I don't know,' he snapped. 'Other women don't seem to make such a palaver about it. The most natural thing in the world.'

'What other women?' she said, incredulous, half laughing.

'Italian women.' He stopped in his tracks. 'For instance. They just get on with it. Look at them now. Che sera sera.'

'When did you get like this?' marvelled Geraldine.

'That's the trouble with you,' said Paul venomously. 'So keen on autonomy. So – so life-denying.'

'Now look here,' said Geraldine. 'You've gone wildly Lawrentian during this holiday and it's *ridiculous*.'

'It *is* part of life, though,' he snapped. 'You can't just say, no thank you.'

'I *am* on the side of life,' she protested. 'Far more than you are.'

'So you keep saying,' he sneered. 'Yours perhaps. Not anybody else's.'

Just then a crowd of babbling children surrounded them, shoving sheets of cardboard at them with knifing movements, jostling, chanting, feeling for their pockets, bright-eyed as birds.

'Ah, get away!' cried Paul, flailing helplessly. 'Vamoose! Leave us alone!'

The children surged against them, attacking and plucking and screeching, warm greedy fingers inside their pockets, dozens of fleshy little starfish hands reaching out. Then, pronto, the infant pack swarmed off, its retreat as instant as its attack, down an adjacent alleyway.

'They took my sunglasses,' said Geraldine. She was unreasonably upset, to the point of tears. A dull red line appeared round the edge of her mouth and she started to sniff. 'Did you see, some of them didn't have shoes on.'

'Like soldier ants,' said Paul, checking his pockets. 'Couldn't do a thing about it, either. They didn't get my wallet. Come on. I'll buy us a drink.'

'Wait a moment,' she said, dragging a knuckle across each of her eyes in turn. 'Do I look all right?'

'Yes,' he said, checking his watch.

In a dark bar lined with mirrors in a turning off the Piazza del Popolo, they stood at the counter and sipped cold beer alongside a handful of silent Italian men.

Paul said, 'I know I'm right.'

Geraldine caught sight of her reflection behind a row of brandy bottles. She looked swollen and green.

'You're such a consumer,' he continued. 'Such a wasteful throw-away artist. Fresh starts and blank screens – they're nonsensical concepts. The last five years, you can't just wipe them, you know.'

'Look, Paul,' she said carefully, after a long pause. 'It's all burnt out. You can see that. It's obvious. You're throwing *putti* onto the embers to try and revive them.'

'Don't,' he said, pulling her round against him, cradling her, his hands clasped over her stomach. 'Don't talk.'

'This holiday has been the decline and fall,' she said, styptic, relieved to be saying it but already full of dismay as the end of their five years together hurtled towards them like a juggernaut.

'No,' he sighed.

'Ciabbata and silly games,' she said. Her throat felt tight.

'We've still got passion,' he insisted, fingering a heather-coloured bruise on her forearm.

'That's not passion,' she said coldly. 'That's just nastiness.'

'What if you *are*, though?' Paul persisted. He smiled. 'Think of last night,' he said in a lower voice. 'How can you say it's over. In fact –' he patted her stomach – 'it might just be starting. Our *vita nuova*.'

She pulled away from him and hid her face behind her hand and the beer glass, letting her hair fall forward in two protective wings. Her knees and ankles were throbbing weakly, tingling, in fact so were all her joints. A gust of heat rushed through her, over her skin and away. Thoughts scrabbled like panicking rabbits, rising in a cyclonic swarm, until she thought the top of her head would take off like a helicopter.

'Don't cry,' he said as the tears fell in her beer.

'I'm not,' she said. 'I imagine it's just the hormones. You know. Women.'

She put on his sunglasses.

'Il gabinetto?' she asked the barman, and walked unsteadily off towards the back of the bar.

On her return she was radiant. Her face was alive and flickering with little smiles, like a fountain. He thought, so that's that, and felt surprisingly detached about it for a moment. She handed his sunglasses back to him, and said, 'It's all right.'

'What's all right?' he asked.

She leaned forward and dropped a syllable into his ear.

'Ah,' he said, and looked down at his hands lying in front of him on the marble counter like rubble.

'Blood,' she said again, softly, exultantly, woundingly.

'Thank God,' she said, more loudly.

And she drained her glass before unleashing a glad unexpected guffaw which had all the men turning to stare.

To Her
Unready Boyfriend

If time sprawled ahead of us in a limitless and improving vista, your reluctance to consider the future wouldn't matter a scrap. We could lie in bed all afternoon browsing through the atlas to map out our itinerary for the next couple of decades or so.

We would discuss the politics of regions shaded in fondant pink and yellow and pistachio, skip to and fro across the equator, splash through the Tasman and Caspian seas, try our tongues round Kandy, Changchun, La Paz, Minsk. I would see you, racoon-furred and seal-booted in the winds of Nova Scotia, paddling our canoe from Natashquan to Sept-Iles, where we would disembark and joyfully climb up to and across the Otish mountains. At the ancient stadium of Olympia, to the susurrous applause of silver leaves we would take our marks on the line where Greek athletes crouched two thousand years ago, then race each other across a hundred yards, repeatedly. Our love would keep us young, along with the avoidance of strong sunlight. We would keep our options open.

Your fondness for dubiety, the way you prize the fluid and infinite possibilities which unfurl before an unattached person, these I sympathize with utterly. You cry freedom and I hear you. Harbouring the sense that there's an epiphany just around the corner, you wait, breath bated, creatively passive, for the chance phrase or glance that will crystallize it all, show you what your life is about and where it is leading. You lack the desire to commit yourself. You tell me you are not ready for the responsibility of a child, and why *should* you be, my darling? You're only thirty-six.

We have loved each other for over ten years now, but the night we met for the first time is like a photograph I carry in my wallet, clear as clear. I sat there in the White Hart, one of a group round a crowded table in a cloud of smoke. We hadn't spoken, you hadn't even seen me, but I was smitten by your heroic frowning profile, the stream of talk (of which I remember not one word, but it was in some way didactic, exhortatory), the glowing cigarette and your excitable hands transferring it to and from your mouth between castles of rhetoric. I wasn't particularly interested in what you were saying, but I wanted to be near you in the way I want to be near a successful log fire. I felt this so strongly I was afraid it would show, so I kept my eyes down, strictly away from your glamorous felty greatcoat, I adjusted my movement as my body swivelled towards you, heliotropic, like a plant towards the sun.

You got up and went to the bar for a round of drinks. Everyone else carried on talking, took no notice. To me it was as if a tooth had been pulled. By your place at the table was an overflowing ashtray and the box of matches you'd been using. I don't smoke. I leaned over, oh so casually, and hooked up that box of matches. I hid it in my hand, a gentle fist around it. Later I examined my trophy in private, sniffed the gunpowder smell and pushed out the miniature drawer with my thumb. Then I struck one of the precious batons and let the flame burn down until it reached my fingers. Ouch.

Since then you have rowed your boat less than merrily and with increasing lassitude down the stream of time. As long as outside events, not personal choice, make things happen, you can accept change with a good enough grace. Staying passive, you reason, is as though you haven't made a choice and your central purity is untouched.

Another woman might start to dream of accidents.

But imagine, just imagine if time were to dawdle and lose itself, as I wish it would; if the laws of mutability were to go a little bit haywire in our case; then perhaps one tender blue-grey evening in the third millennium we might find ourselves sitting by the fireside in our late fifties, our eyes would meet, and we would know we were ready at last. Our mortgage would be negligible by then, your thesis would at last be lapped in gold-tooled leather, and the worst of our wanderlust would have been slaked. Hand in hand we would climb the stairs that night to start a baby. And not before.

For, my dear love, you deserve acres of time, long red carpets of it; nor would I wish any less for you.

But, my sweet eternal boy, in recent months I've been dogged by a rhythmic noise, soft but distinct, tick-*tock*, tick-*tock* like the crocodile in Peter Pan. I've reached a certain age, you must remember, and this wretched clock noise, which increases in volume as the day progresses and is at its most distracting, menacing even, just when I'm undressing for bed, warns me, *Get*-a-move-on *hur*ry-up, *Get*-a-move-on *not*-much-time.

It's all right for you, you're like the popes in the Renaissance, you can go on fathering children till you're eighty-three. But if you want us to stay together, and I say this as one who as you know has never used emotional blackmail in all our years together, if you want us to stay together, I say, then you must start telling the time by my clock. I can't ignore it.

You may prefer, of course, to wait another ten or fifteen years, as in my fireside fantasy. You may prefer to wait for the arrival of a paunch and root canal work before at last sowing the long-hoarded seed. If so, I won't be there. I'll be somewhere else, giggling with my adolescent daughter.

You say, our love for each other is enough, my talk is dangerously hubristic, let's take each day as it comes.

The trouble with that is, whether we like it or not we can't stay the same. It's not allowed. There's no procedure for freezing our present happiness, no insurance scheme against future grief or coldness and misunderstanding.

We can't mark time ad infinitum. Meanwhile, to our dismay, this baby denial will start to appear increasingly as a match that's not been struck. The irony is that you're the one who goes on about death all the time. What's it all about? Is there just nothing at the end? Can't you see this is your one sure way of cocking a snook at all that? All right, eventually, I admit, you will be forced by the laws of physics to unlink your molecules, to crumble into motes and spores and polycarbons, and your strongest comfort is that you might with luck become part of the atmosphere. But if your child is at the bedside when you draw your last breath, a child with your hunted look, your heroic profile, new-minted, then the baton will have been passed on.

A child would alter the balance between us, a child would turn the direction of our eyes away from the withering and fattening of our over-familiar selves towards the pleasure of a fresh new presence growing.

Forgive me for pointing this out, my love, but there is something lugubrious and loose-endish about you, a central glumness that my charming presence hasn't managed to melt entirely. You can warm your hands at the fire of other people's high jinks, but in your own kitchen there is a sadness, as of an uncooked cake. You're unfinished, some sort of refugee, abandoned early on and – despite my best efforts – not yet rescued.

You're wonderfully perspicacious, irresistibly beautiful, and you say I've pulled you out of the miseries that used to plague you. I can however only do so much for you; some mothering of course; but I am *not* your mother.

I would *like* to be a mother, not yours but still a mother. For this, though, I want your consent.

See me through nine months. I want to be a nice ripe pear on the sun-warmed bricks of a walled garden.

He'd look just like you. He could curl up in the crook of your arm at night. He'd stare at you in amazement at first, with a dazzled china-blue frown. When he meowed you could pass him over to me, I'd calm him down. I'd do it all, you wouldn't even notice.

Or perhaps we might have a girl, a baby girl, and after hacking through all those tiresome thorn-hedged years you would at last have found your own princess. You are capable of such generous secret tenderness that I think you couldn't fail to be a father both adoring and adored.

Let me see if I can draw a parallel to make you understand. I find it very peculiar that someone so clever can be so obtuse.

Do you remember the last time we saw Susan, just after she'd moved to the little house in Ansty with its south-facing garden, do you remember how she said she was home at last, this was the place she wanted to live in for the rest of her life? And as an acknowledgement of this fact she had planted a mulberry tree, knowing full well that she wouldn't be seeing any fruit on its branches for a good twenty-five years. I liked that. It was an act of faith. I'm fed up with us being so abjectly tentative.

If you carry on trying to rope us together with these massive cables of inertia, we'll fly apart at last. Time won't stand still just because we've been lucky in love, more's the pity.

Now, then: let's move on *now*. Let's abandon our fastidious comforts, wave goodbye to our turtledove snuggery while there's still time. Come on. You can't keep yourself to yourself forever. Be brave! Let's jump before we're pushed.

Come to bed. Unprotected. Now.

Last Orders

She was a bulbous bottle, unreliably stoppered, and any movement away from the strictest upright provoked the genie into shooting acrid slop up to her epiglottis. So she stayed vertical, and when night came propped herself against a bank of bolsters like an Anglo-Saxon afraid of death's approach during sleep.

These night hours unrolled bales of poor but heavy slumber, thick and threadbare like hessian, coarse curtains which fanned open occasionally onto thresholds of glimmering incomprehension. The dreams were of release, violent and half-baked, there was one where she was flat as a flounder with eyes on the same side of her nose, shifting along an inch above the seabed, and then she would wake into the half-light with a strong aversion to duality and everything to do with bifurcation.

This had been a bad night, spiralling down through threats of knives and stomach-globes. The easy tears streaked her cheeks, cheap as dew. She lay and languished, watching the forked radish which was Patrick pulling on its trousers in the gloom.

'Twelve days late now,' she said. 'My body doesn't work.'

'Yes it does,' said Patrick, scrabbling through a dish of loose change. 'Babies come when they're ready.'

'How would *you* know,' she said, turning her big white clumsy face into the pillow.

'The doctors say so,' he said, as usual, strapping on his watch. 'Sorry, got to rush, I'm late.'

'Good luck with the Brisbane blockbuster,' she said. 'Where's lunch?'

'Let The Good Times Roll.'

'You lucky devil.'

'Don't forget we're off to the Bengal Tiger tonight.'

She groaned.

'Worth a try,' he said. 'Whenever anybody hears you're late, they mention hot curry. If it works we'll call him Vindaloo.'

She lay in bed for an hour after he had gone, dipping back into drifts of half-sleep, trawling her memory again for more specific details of the wish-gone-sour tale which surfaced every morning now.

There was a withered old man imploring some ringleted goddess to release him. He had been granted his wish for eternal life, but had forgotten to ask for eternal youth at the same time, and now, as he hobbled across her gleaming marble halls on wrinkled feet, tears trickling down his walnut face and silvery waist-length beard, he pleaded for the ordinary power to die.

Watching the summer light strengthen at the margins of the bedroom curtains, she wondered why this story kept returning to her, since it did not concern birth, but death.

When she started to worry again that her body would never work, that she would simply grow bigger and bigger, then she commenced the laborious business of getting dressed.

The telephone rang.

'*Still* nothing?' came the incredulous voice of her aunt. 'It'll have a beard and long toe-nails by now.'

'Any day,' she said, automatically, as she had been saying for the last month.

Now that the official hospital date, the baby's Estimated Time of Arrival, had come and gone, it was like life after death. Only she had not yet laid down her life. This was limbo. She was not currently living inside real hours and minutes. Perhaps this was what was meant by living on borrowed time. She had run out of credit with her waiting relatives, anyway; they almost jeered at her when they telephoned now. Invalid in both senses of the word, she lumbered out into the little back garden. These days, walking was like wading through sea water up to the thighs.

Bees boomed inside the freckle-throated foxgloves. From the lime trees came a rustle like stiff silk tussore, and a sweet soap-and-talcum-powder smell. Already the garden was a pocket of heat. This was the hottest June for twelve years, as everybody kept saying. There was a menacing innocence, a pre-war stasis about it.

'*Still* not had it?' The old lady who lived next door appeared at the fence, her leech-black eyes peering through the trellis of honeysuckle. 'You must be very worried by now.'

'I'm all right,' she said, taking a step back towards the kitchen door. 'How are you?'

'As you know. Lonely as hell since Reg died,' said Mrs Pightle. 'Sometimes I get so bored I wish even something nasty would happen.'

Wanting to avoid infection by contact with Mrs Pightle's misery, she took another step back.

'Mustn't grumble though,' said Mrs Pightle, eyeing her bulk sharply as though suspecting her of fraudulent practices, a cushion up her teeshirt. Then, unnervingly, she snapped, 'I kill each day as it comes.'

'There's the telephone,' she said, and scuttled back inside.

'*Well?*' came her mother's voice. 'Are you going to tell me you've had it?' She held the receiver at arm's length for a moment, as gingerly as if it had been a scorpion.

Twelve days ago had been the promised day. The flat was perfectly clean for the first time in its life, she had even polished the windows and mirrors; she had piled two pounds of glossy cherries into the green glass dish and had put a vase of straight-backed tulips in each of the rooms. It had felt like her birthday. Patrick had brought home a slice of Brie, almost ripe – 'I thought you might like it for your first meal after the baby,' he had said, 'since you've been complaining for nine months about how you wish you could have a little bit of soft cheese.' He had made her feel like Ben Gunn, whose first request after years of being marooned on a desert island was for some crumbs of toasted cheese. Ben Gunn, too, had had a long beard and toe-nails, she thought confusedly. Later that morning they had gone to the hospital for her forty-week appointment.

The baby's head had not engaged, said the registrar; the absence of Braxton Hicks contractions was absolutely no cause for concern. It'll be a few days yet, he had advised, we'll have to wait for the cervix to ripen; don't look so disappointed, you've got a marvellous haemoglobin count.

A week later the tulips were swooping drunkenly, stems curving in art nouveau arabesques so that their splayed flowerheads touched the dust-gathering surfaces at last, almost inaudibly, and fell to pieces, each petal a glamorous painted coracle. The cherries grew bruised, then rotten. She threw them away. After nine days, when it had lost in form what it had gained in odour, Patrick ate the Brie. She had to dust again, and kicked the bag she had packed for hospital six weeks ago, now standing sad and ridiculous in the corner of the bedroom like a cancelled holiday. At her forty-first-week appointment, they gave her a graph-paper kick-chart to fill in; she ticked a square for each movement the baby made until the tenth square was attained, which was always before midday; and then she had nothing to do except field the phone calls. They told her to be patient, and she gave a wan sneer. She was clearly nothing but a bad joke on two legs, a joke without a punchline.

It was galling now to see the sunny patch of garden through the doorway and know that Mrs Pightle would get her if she put her nose outside. She hadn't been more than five hundred yards from the house for more than a fortnight now, so convinced had she been that the baby would appear at its appointed time to the sound of empyreal trumpets, trailing clouds of glory. She had refused plans to meet anyone because they might have to be cancelled, and her only contact with the outside world for the last fortnight had been via the telephone wire and Patrick, or from sending out letters like messages in bottles. Prevented by Mrs Pightle from watching the grass grow, she had instead monitored the progress of her nail and hair lengths, like Rapunzel waiting for rescue from the witch's tower.

She sat down with her book on How to Have a Baby, and the baby inside her woke up and started its bulging movements. It, too, was a prisoner in a tower, of course. They were in a double bind. Strange, to be lounging around in this summer torpor, lazy as an aquarium, while just round the corner waited bloody scenes of violence and danger and life at its most portentous.

The telephone rang.

'Are you still in one piece? Never mind, they're bound to induce now. Make the most of your last days – this is the last time alone you'll ever have. I haven't had a minute to myself since Maisie was born. And remember, the first six weeks are *awful*. Impossible to describe, but *you'll* see. It's *chaos*. It gets better gradually. After about a year. Have you tried sitting on a washing machine during the spin cycle?'

She went back to her book and looked up induction in the index. 'The doctor snags a hole in the membranes which surround your baby with an instrument like a long crochet hook, then the waters gush out,' she read.

She went to the bookcase and pulled out an old exercise book. A long time ago she had copied out a poem written in the Tower of London by a man who knew he was going to be executed the next morning. Here it was, and it was by twenty-six-year-old Chidiock Tichbourne whose head was scythed from his trunk in 1586 before he had had time to write much at all.

> My prime of youth is but a frost of cares;
> My feast of joy is but a dish of pain;
> My crop of corn is but a field of tares;
> And all my good is but vain hope of gain:
> The day is past, and yet I saw no sun;
> And now I live, and now my life is done.

I'll never see Mexico, she thought, the jointed armadillo running across the sand. I won't be able to try hang-gliding in case I leave an orphan. I haven't *done* anything yet.

> My tale was heard, and yet it was not told;
> My fruit is fall'n, and yet my leaves are green;
> My youth is spent, and yet I am not old;
> I saw the world, and yet I was not seen:
> My thread is cut, and yet it is not spun;
> And now I live, and now my life is done.

The telephone rang. It was Patrick, calling from a phone box on his way to lunch.

'Do we *want* a baby?' she asked.

'Of course we do! More than anything else in the world! I'm so happy I'm almost scared.'

'I never seem to feel the right thing at the right time. I'm unnatural.'

'No you're not. But it'll be all right, you'll see. Have you any *idea* how much I love you? You're mine now.'

The pips went and she used this as an excuse to put the phone down. She heard herself swearing and cursing.

'Hormones,' she said flatly.

> I sought my death, and found it in my womb;
> I looked for life, and saw it was a shade;
> I trod the earth, and knew it was my tomb;
> And now I die, and now I was but made:
> My glass is full, and now my glass is run;
> And now I live, and now my life is done.

The telephone rang again.

'It's Wendy here, *you* know, from the antenatal class. Just ringing to let you know I've had it. It's a boy, eight pounds six ounces. I know, he wasn't due for another two weeks, but he couldn't wait, could he. Funny really, even though he'll be older than yours now, when you think about it yours has actually been *alive* a whole month longer . . . What was it like? Do you *really* want to know? I don't think I should tell you. Oh, all right. It was horrible, not a bit like the classes said. At least it was quick, well, eight hours. I started getting pains about two forty-five on Saturday. Geoff wanted to go off to the gym for his circuit training, and by the time he got back I said, this is it, we've got to go to hospital. Anyway I don't think I'll go into details with you in your condition – I'm so glad *I* wasn't late, I couldn't bear it – but don't believe them when they say it doesn't hurt. I was screaming my head off at the end. Then it shot out at ten-fifty p.m. I remember Geoff said, just in time for last orders.'

Come pain, welcome pain, she thought as she put the phone down. I want to be cool and free again, lean and Atlantic-salted. I want to lose this fish-like full-throated extra under the chin. I wish I could run like the wind across

frost-crusted grass, or lunge and bump at will in the night.
I want to say goodbye to this batwing mask of pregnancy
across my nose and cheeks.

The telephone rang. It was Wendy again, suggesting
that she drive at thirty miles an hour over sleeping
policemen since this had worked for the woman in the bed
next to hers at St Mary's, and she had been two weeks
overdue.

Taking up another baby book, emotional rather than
technical this time, along with a handful of raisins for
lunch, she read, 'When you refuse to leave your breast-fed
baby with a bottle and a sitter in order to go out and enjoy
yourself, it isn't self-sacrifice but self-protection. While
you and your baby are interlocked in this way, you can
only be happy if she is happy.' She let the book rest in her
lap and stared hungrily at the open door. This was what
people had said before when she had voiced doubts about
missing pubs, parties, dancing, travel; they always smiled
as though she were odd or innocent, and said, 'You'll see;
you won't *want* to.'

You will not be you any more, her ego told her id. Not
only will you have produced somebody else from inside
you, someone quite different and separate, but you
yourself will change into somebody quite different, overnight – a Mother.

Her id held its sides and screeched with laughter. Pull
the other one! it pleaded, weak with mirth.

What if she failed to feel misery at the thought of a bottle
and a sitter? What if they seemed fair exchange for a bottle
and a party? *Would* she feel the necessary 'interlock' that
would turn her into a stay-at-home?

Thinking back to that last outing a month ago, she saw it had been, among other things, a wake for her old self. She had taken a valedictory taxi back to the flat, sitting upright on the high-backed seat in the purring darkness, exhausted by the baby beating away in protest since early evening, but humming and happy too.

'Enjoy yourself while you can,' said the taxi driver over his shoulder. He was the cold, light-eyed virile sort with steely grey hair and an air of grim fitness.

'Oh, that was the last party for a while,' she had said airily. 'I'm about to have a baby. Have *you* got any children?'

'I wish I'd drowned them at birth,' he had said. 'Look at it like this. Two people get together, they get on well. Out to the cinema, out to the pub, go to bed together; out to the pub. Then the little bleeder arrives. It's meant to bring you closer together, but does it? Does it ****. *You* say, let's go down the pub. *She* says, ooh no, the baby's feeding pattern, or something like that. She says, *you* go down the pub. Nah, you say. You sit around a bit. Then you think, OK, just for half an hour. So you're down there, you think, well, this is fun, it's a bit lively. Next thing you're talking to someone who's *not* the old lady. And you hear people say they bring you closer together! Still, not a lot you can do about it at this stage in the game by the look of you. Tell you what, I'll give you a tip. Give it a few spoons of Benelux – not too often – just when you really need a couple of hours' peace. Night Nurse is too strong.'

Well, she was going out tonight, wasn't she. 'Positively my last appearance,' she muttered. 'Like some old music hall star who doesn't know when to call it a day.'

Patrick brought home the Australian author whom he had taken out to lunch. They both had the withered eyelids and kamikaze air of people who have been drinking during daylight and who intend to go on against their better judgement.

'Hope you don't mind,' whispered Patrick. 'I meant to ring and warn you, but he's been like a limpet and he keeps on telling me how he doesn't know anybody in London.'

'The more the merrier,' she yawned. They shuffled off down the road to the Bengal Tiger, the men creeping along to keep her company, one on either side, like the ceremonial escort of an ancient monarch.

Once on the threshold of the restaurant she looked around ravenously at this fresh landscape, noticing that all eyes skidded off her bulk and that she had become a visual embarrassment now she was out in public after so long. She did not care. It was somewhere different. She admired the filigree metal of the basket holding poppadoms, and watched Patrick and his author devouring stuffed paratha. They were discussing differences in national humour, comparing Australian with English.

'Ours is a bit cruder, a bit brasher,' said the Australian earnestly, popping an onion bhaji whole into his mouth. 'Our jokes are not exactly subtle. For example, would you find this funny? I do, but my humour is very Antipodean.'

Patrick cocked his ear in the attitude of one about to enjoy a treat.

'Well, here's Sheila and she's standing on the edge of Sydney Suspension bridge and she's about to jump off. Bruce comes running up, all concern, shouts, "Why Sheila, *why*?'' ''Because I'm pregnant,'' says Sheila. ''Jeez, Sheila,'' says Bruce, 'not only are you a bloody good lay but you're a bloody good sport too, Sheila.'' Now you either find that funny or you don't.'

Patrick was looking at her uneasily, but she liked a joke, even an ideologically unsound joke, and she was sniggering into her chicken dhansak.

Relieved, Patrick laughed and crowed and said, 'Well, have *you* heard the one about the man who's drinking alone in a pub and he wants to go off and have a pee, but he's scared someone'll steal his pint, so he props a little note against it saying, ''I have spat in this beer.'' '

'No,' said the Australian, grinning attentively and gulping lager.

'When he gets back from the Gents his beer's still there – but somebody's scribbled, ''So have I,'' on the note. Ha, ha, ha!'

The two men rocked with laughter. To her surprise, she was prickling with alarm. She heard his voice again down the telephone: 'You're *mine* now.' The baby heaved up against her ribs like a barge. She restrained herself from lifting Patrick's pint and pouring it over his head.

'Excuse me,' she said, the syllables glacial in her burning mouth; and waddled off down a spiral staircase to the Ladies.

There, she locked herself into a cubicle and leant her forehead against the gleaming marble-tiled walls, and wept, and swore, and pleaded for release.

Heavy Weather

'You should never have married me.'

'I haven't regretted it for an instant.'

'Not *you*, you fool! *Me!* You shouldn't have got me to marry you if you loved me. Why *did* you, when you knew it would let me in for all *this*. It's not *fair!*'

'I didn't know. I know it's not. But what can I do about it?'

'I'm being mashed up and eaten alive.'

'I know. I'm sorry.'

'It's not your fault. But what can I do?'

'I don't know.'

So the conversation had gone last night in bed, followed by platonic embraces. They were on ice at the moment, so far as anything further was concerned. The smoothness and sweet smell of their children, the baby's densely packed pearly limbs, the freshness of the little girl's breath when she yawned, these combined to accentuate the grossness of their own bodies. They eyed each other's mooching adult bulk with mutual lack of enthusiasm, and fell asleep.

At four in the morning, the baby was punching and shouting in his Moses basket. Frances forced herself awake, lying for the first moments like a flattened boxer in the ring trying to rise while the count was made. She got up and fell over, got up again and scooped Matthew from the basket. He was huffing with eagerness, and scrabbled crazily at her breasts like a drowning man until she lay down with him. A few seconds more and he had abandoned himself to rhythmic gulping. She stroked his soft head and drifted off. When she woke again, it was six o'clock and he was sleeping between her and Jonathan.

For once, nobody was touching her. Like Holland she lay, aware of a heavy ocean at her seawall, its weight poised to race across the low country.

The baby was now three months old, and she had not had more than half an hour alone in the twenty-four since his birth in February. He was big and hungry and needed her there constantly on tap. Also, his two-year-old sister Lorna was, unwillingly, murderously jealous, which made everything much more difficult. This time round was harder, too, because when one was asleep the other would be awake and vice versa. If only she could get them to nap at the same time, Frances started fretting, then she might be able to sleep for some minutes during the day and that would get her through. But they wouldn't, and she couldn't. She had taken to muttering I can't bear it, I can't bear it, without realizing she was doing so until she heard Lorna chanting I can't bear it! I can't bear it! as she skipped along beside the pram, and this made her blush with shame at her own weediness.

Now they were all four in Dorset for a week's holiday.

The thought of having to organize all the food, sheets, milk, baths and nappies made her want to vomit.

In her next chunk of sleep came that recent nightmare, where men with knives and scissors advanced on the felled trunk which was her body.

'How would you like it?' she said to Jonathan. 'It's like a doctor saying, now we're just going to snip your scrotum in half, but don't worry, it mends very well down there, we'll stitch you up and you'll be fine.'

It was gone seven by now, and Lorna was leaning on the bars of her cot like Farmer Giles, sucking her thumb in a ruminative pipe-smoking way. The room stank like a lion house. She beamed as her mother came in and lifted her arms up. Frances hoisted her into the bath, stripped her down and detached the dense brown nappy from between her knees. Lorna carolled, 'I can sing a *rain*bow,' raising her faint fine eyebrows at the high note, graceful and perfect, as her mother sluiced her down with jugs of water.

'Why does everything take so *long*?' moaned Jonathan. 'It only takes *me* five minutes to get ready.'

Frances did not bother to answer. She was sagging with the effortful boredom of assembling the paraphernalia needed for a morning out in the car. Juice. Beaker with screw-on lid. Flannels. Towels. Changes of clothes in case of car sickness. Nappies. Rattle. Clean muslins to catch Matthew's curdy regurgitations. There was more. What was it?

'Oh, come on, Jonathan, think,' she said. 'I'm fed up with having to plan it all.'

'What do you think I've been doing for the last hour?' he

shouted. 'Who was it that changed Matthew's nappy just now? Eh?'

'Congratulations,' she said. 'Don't shout or I'll cry.'

Lorna burst into tears.

'Why is everywhere always such a *mess*,' said Jonathan, picking up plastic spiders, dinosaurs, telephones, beads and bears, his grim scowl over the mound of primary colours like a traitor's head on a platter of fruit.

'I *want* dat spider, Daddy!' screamed Lorna. 'Give it to me!'

During the ensuing struggle, Frances pondered her tiredness. Her muscles twitched as though they had been tenderized with a steak bat. There was a bar of iron in the back of her neck, and she felt unpleasantly weightless in the cranium, a gin-drinking side effect without the previous fun. The year following the arrival of the first baby had gone in pure astonishment at the loss of freedom, but second time round it was spinning away in exhaustion. Matthew woke at one a.m. and four a.m., and Lorna at six-thirty a.m. During the days, fatigue came at her in concentrated doses, like a series of time bombs.

'Are we ready at last?' said Jonathan, breathing heavily. 'Are we ready to go?'

'Um, nearly,' said Frances. 'Matthew's making noises. I think I'd better feed him, or else I'll end up doing it in a lay-by.'

'Right,' said Jonathan. 'Right.'

Frances picked up the baby. 'What a nice fat parcel you are,' she murmured in his delighted ear. 'Come on, my love.'

'Matthew's not your love,' said Lorna. '*I'm* your love. You say, C'mon love, to *me*.'

'You're *both* my loves,' said Frances.

The baby was shaking with eagerness, and pouted his mouth as she pulled her shirt up. The little girl sat down beside her, pulled up her own teeshirt and applied a teddy bear to her nipple. She grinned at her mother.

Frances looked down at Matthew's head, which was shaped like a brick or a small wholemeal loaf, and remembered again how it had come down through the middle of her. She was trying very hard to lose her awareness of this fact, but it would keep re-presenting itself.

'D'you know,' said Lorna, free hand held palm upwards, hyphen eyebrows lifting, 'd'you know, I was sucking my thumb when I was coming downstairs, mum, mum, then my foot slipped and my thumb came out of my mouth.'

'Well, that's very interesting, Lorna,' said Frances.

Two minutes later, Lorna caught the baby's head a ringing smack and ran off. Jonathan watched as Frances lunged clumsily after her, the baby jouncing at her breast, her stained and crumpled shirt undone, her hair a bird's nest, her face craggy with fatigue, and found himself dubbing the tableau, Portrait of rural squalor in the manner of William Hogarth. He bent to put on his shoes, stuck his right foot in first then pulled it out as though bitten.

'What's *that*,' he said in tones of profound disgust. He held his shoe in front of Frances's face.

'It looks like baby sick,' she said. 'Don't look at me. It's not my fault.'

'It's all so bloody *basic*,' said Jonathan, breathing hard, hopping off towards the kitchen.

'If you think that's basic, try being me,' muttered Frances. 'You don't know what basic *means*.'

'Daddy put his foot in Matthew's sick,' commented Lorna, laughing heartily.

At Cerne Abbas they stood and stared across at the chalky white outline of the Iron-Age giant cut into the green hill.

'It's enormous, isn't it,' said Frances.

'Do you remember when we went to stand on it?' said Jonathan. 'On that holiday in Child Okeford five years ago?'

'Of course,' said Frances. She saw the ghosts of their frisky former selves running around the giant's limbs and up onto his phallus. Nostalgia filled her eyes and stabbed her smartly in the guts.

'The woman riding high above with bright hair flapping free,' quoted Jonathan. 'Will you be able to grow *your* hair again?'

'Yes, yes. Don't look at me like that, though. I know I look like hell.'

A month before this boy was born, Frances had had her hair cut short. Her head had looked like a pea on a drum. It still did. With each pregnancy, her looks had hurtled five years on. She had started using sentences beginning, 'When I was young.' Ah, youth! Idleness! Sleep! How pleasant it had been to play the centre of her own stage.

And how disorientating was this overnight demotion from Brünnhilde to spear-carrier.

'What's that,' said Lorna. 'That *thing*.'

'It's a giant,' said Frances.

'Like in Jacknabeanstork?'

'Yes.'

'But what's that *thing*. That thing on the giant.'

'It's the giant's thing.'

'Is it his stick thing?'

'Yes.'

'My baby budder's got a stick thing.'

'Yes.'

'But I haven't got a stick thing.'

'No.'

'Daddy's got a stick thing.'

'Yes.'

'But *Mummy* hasn't got a stick thing. We're the same, Mummy.'

She beamed and put her warm paw in Frances's.

'You can't see round without an appointment,' said the keeper of Hardy's cottage. 'You should have telephoned.'

'We did,' bluffed Jonathan. 'There was no answer.'

'When was that?'

'Twenty to ten this morning.'

'Hmph. I was over sorting out some trouble at Clouds Hill. T. E. Lawrence's place. All right, you can go through. But keep them under control, won't you.'

They moved slowly through the low-ceilinged rooms, whispering to impress the importance of good behaviour on Lorna.

'This is the room where he was born,' said Jonathan, at the head of the stairs.

'Do you remember from when we visited last time?' said Frances slowly. 'It's coming back to me. He was his mother's first child, she nearly died in labour, then the doctor thought the baby was dead and threw him into a basket while he looked after the mother. But the midwife noticed he was breathing.'

'Then he carried on till he was eighty-seven,' said Jonathan.

They clattered across the old chestnut floorboards, on into another little bedroom with deep thick-walled windowseats.

'Which one's your favourite now?' asked Frances.

'Oh, still *Jude the Obscure*, I think,' said Jonathan. 'The tragedy of unfulfilled aims. Same for anyone first generation at university.'

'Poor Jude, laid low by pregnancy,' said Frances. 'Another victim of biology as destiny.'

'Don't *talk*, you two,' said Lorna.

'At least Sue and Jude aimed for friendship as well as all the other stuff,' said Jonathan.

'Unfortunately, all the other stuff made friendship impossible, didn't it,' said Frances.

'Don't *talk*!' shouted Lorna.

'Don't shout!' said Jonathan. Lorna fixed him with a calculating blue eye and produced an ear-splitting scream. The baby jerked in his arms and started to howl.

'Hardy didn't have children, did he,' said Jonathan above the din. 'I'll take them outside, I've seen enough. You stay up here a bit longer if you want to.'

Frances stood alone in the luxury of the empty room and shuddered. She moved around the furniture and thought fond savage thoughts of silence in the cloisters of a convent, a blessed place where all was monochrome and non-viscous. Sidling up unprepared to a mirror on the wall she gave a yelp at her reflection. The skin was the colour and texture of pumice stone, the grim jaw set like a lion's muzzle. And the eyes, the eyes far back in the skull were those of a herring three days dead.

Jonathan was sitting with the baby on his lap by a row of lupins and marigolds, reading to Lorna from a newly acquired guide book.

'When Thomas was a little boy he knelt down one day in a field and began eating grass to see what it was like to be a sheep.'

'What did the sheep say?' asked Lorna.

'The sheep said, er, so now you know.'

'And what else?'

'Nothing else.'

'Why?'

'What do you mean, why?'

'*Why?*'

'Look,' he said when he saw Frances. 'I've bought a copy of *Jude the Obscure* too, so we can read to each other when we've got a spare moment.'

'Spare moment!' said Frances. 'But how lovely you look with the children at your knees, the roses round the cottage door. How I would like to be the one coming back from work to find you all bathed and brushed, and a hot meal in the oven and me unwinding with a glass of beer in a hard-earned crusty glow of righteousness.'

'*I* don't get that,' Jonathan reminded her.

'That's because I can't do it properly yet,' said Frances. 'But, still, I wish it could be the other way round. Or at least, half and half. And I was thinking, what a cheesy business Eng. Lit. is, all those old men peddling us lies about life and love. They never get as far as this bit, do they.'

'Thomas 1840, Mary 1842, Henry 1851, Kate 1856,' read Jonathan. 'Perhaps we could have two more.'

'I'd kill myself,' said Frances.

'What's the matter with you?' said Jonathan to Matthew, who was grizzling and struggling in his arms.

'I think I'll have to feed him again,' said Frances.

'What, already?'

'It's nearly two hours.'

'Hey, you can't do that here,' said the custodian, appearing at their bench like a bad fairy. 'We have visitors from all over the world here. Particularly from Japan. The Japanese are a very modest people. And they don't come all this way to see THAT sort of thing.'

'It's a perfectly natural function,' said Jonathan.

'So's going to the lavatory!' said the custodian.

'Is it all right if I take him over behind those hollyhocks?' asked Frances. 'Nobody could possibly see me there. It's just, in this heat he won't feed if I try to do it in the car.'

The custodian snorted and stumped back to his lair.

Above the thatched roof the huge and gentle trees rustled hundreds of years' worth of leaves in the pre-storm stir. Frances shrugged, heaved Matthew up so that his socks dangled on her hastily covered breast, and retreated to the hollyhock screen. As he fed, she observed the green-tinged light in the garden, the crouching cat over in a bed of limp snapdragons, and registered the way things look before an onslaught, defenceless and excited, tense and passive. She thought of Bathsheba Everdene at bay, crouching in the bed of ferns.

When would she be able to read a book again? In life before the children, she had read books on the bus, in the bathroom, in bed, while eating, through television, under radio noise, in cafés. Now, if she picked one up, Lorna shouted, 'Stop reading, Mummy,' and pulled her by the nose until she was looking into her small cross face.

Jonathan meandered among the flowerbeds flicking through *Jude the Obscure*, Lorna snapping and shouting at his heels. He was ignoring her, and Frances could see he had already bought a tantrum since Lorna was now entered into one of the stretches of the day when her self-control flagged and fled. She sighed like Cassandra but didn't have the energy to nag as he came towards her.

'Listen to this,' Jonathan said, reading from *Jude the Obscure*. ' "Time and circumstance, which enlarge the views of most men, narrow the views of women almost invariably." '

'Is it any bloody wonder,' said Frances.

'I want you to *play* with me, Daddy,' whined Lorna.

'Bit of a sexist remark, though, eh?' said Jonathan.

'Bit of a sexist process, you twit,' said Frances.

Lorna gave Matthew a tug which almost had him on the ground. Torn from his milky trance, he quavered, horror-struck, for a moment, then, as Frances braced herself, squared his mouth and started to bellow.

Jonathan seized Lorna, who became as rigid as a steel

girder, and swung her high up above his head. The air was split with screams.

'Give her to me,' mouthed Frances across the awe-inspiring noise.

'She's a noise terrorist,' shouted Jonathan.

'Oh, please let me have her,' said Frances.

'You shouldn't give in to her,' said po-faced Jonathan, handing over the flailing parcel of limbs.

'Lorna, sweetheart, look at me,' said Frances.

'Naaoow!' screamed Lorna.

'Shshush,' said Frances. 'Tell me what's the matter.'

Lorna poured out a flood of incomprehensible complaint, raving like a chimpanzee. At one point, Frances deciphered, 'You always feed MATTHEW.'

'You should *love* your baby brother,' interposed Jonathan.

'You can't tell her she *ought* to love anybody,' snapped Frances. 'You can tell her she must behave properly, but you can't tell her what to feel. Look, Lorna,' she continued, exercising her favourite distraction technique. 'The old man is coming back. He's cross with us. Let's run away.'

Lorna turned her streaming eyes and nose in the direction of the custodian, who was indeed hotfooting it across the lawn towards them, and tugged her mother's hand. The two of them lurched off, Frances buttoning herself up as she went.

They found themselves corralled into a cement area at the back of the Smuggler's Arms, a separate space where young family pariahs like themselves could bicker over fish fingers. Waiting at the bar, Jonathan observed the comfortable tables inside, with their noisy laughing groups of the energetic elderly tucking into plates of gammon and plaice and profiteroles.

'Just look at them,' said the crumpled man beside him, who was paying for a trayload of Fanta and baked beans. 'Skipped the war. Nil unemployment, home in time for tea.' He took a great gulp of lager. 'Left us to scream in our prams, screwed us up good and proper. When our kids come along, what happens? You don't see the grandparents for dust, that's what happens. They're all off out enjoying themselves, kicking the prams out the way with their Hush Puppies, spending the money like there's no tomorrow.'

Jonathan grunted uneasily. He still could not get used to the way he found himself involved in intricate conversations with complete strangers, incisive, frank, frequently desperate, whenever he was out with Frances and the children. It used to be only women who talked like that, but now, among parents of young children, it seemed to have spread across the board.

Frances was trying to allow the baby to finish his recent interrupted feed as discreetly as she could, while watching Lorna move inquisitively among the various family groups. She saw her go up to a haggard woman changing a nappy beside a trough of geraniums.

'Your baby's got a stick thing like my baby budder.' Lorna's piercing voice soared above the babble. 'I haven't got a stick thing cos I'm a little gel. My mummy's got fur on her potim.'

Frances abandoned their table and made her way over to the geranium trough.

'Sorry if she's been getting in your way,' she said to the woman.

'Chatty, isn't she,' commented the woman unenthusiastically. 'How many have you got?'

'Two. I'm shattered.'

'The third's the killer.'

'That's my baby budder,' said Lorna, pointing at Matthew.

'He's a big boy,' said the woman. 'What did he weigh when he came out?'

'Ten pounds.'

'Just like a turkey,' she said, disgustingly, and added, 'Mine were whoppers too. They all had to be cut out of me, one way or the other.'

By the time they returned to the cottage, the air was weighing on them like blankets. Each little room was an envelope of pressure. Jonathan watched Frances collapse into a chair with children all over her. Before babies, they had been well matched. Then, with the arrival of their first child, it had been a case of Woman Overboard. He'd watched, ineffectual but sympathetic, trying to keep her cheerful as she clung onto the edge of the raft, holding out weevil-free biscuits for her to nibble, and all the time she gazed at him with appalled eyes. Just as they had grown used to this state, difficult but tenable, and were even managing to start hauling her on board again an inch at a time, just as she had her elbows up on the raft and they were congratulating themselves with a kiss, well, along came the second baby in a great slap of a wave that drove her off the raft altogether. Now she was out there in the sea while he bobbed up and down, forlorn but more or less dry, and watched her face between its two satellites dwindling to the size of a fist, then to a plum, and at last to a mere speck of plankton. He dismissed it from his mind.

'I'll see if I can get the shopping before the rain starts,' he said, dashing out to the car again, knee-deep in cow parsley.

'You really should keep an eye on how much bread we've got left,' he called earnestly as he unlocked the car. 'It won't be *my* fault if I'm struck by lightning.'

There was the crumpling noise of thunder, and silver cracked the sky. Frances stood in the doorway holding the baby, while Lorna clawed and clamoured at her to be held in her free arm.

'Oh, Lorna,' said Frances, hit by a wave of bone-aching fatigue. 'You're too heavy, my sweet.' She closed the cottage door as Lorna started to scream, and stood looking down at her with something like fear. She saw a miniature fee-fi-fo-fum creature working its way through a pack of adults, chewing them up and spitting their bones out.

'Come into the back room, Lorna, and I'll read you a book while I feed Matthew.'

'I don't want to.'

'Why don't you want to?'

'I just don't want to.'

'Can't you tell me why?'

'Do you know, I just don't WANT to!'

'All right, *dear*. I'll feed him on my own then.'

'NO!' screamed Lorna. 'PUT HIM IN DA BIN! HE'S RUBBISH!'

'Don't scream, you little beast,' said Frances hopelessly, while the baby squared his mouth and joined in the noise.

Lorna turned the volume up and waited for her to crack. Frances walked off to the kitchen with the baby and quickly closed the door. Lorna gave a howl of rage from the other side and started to smash at it with fists and toys. Children were petal-skinned ogres, Frances realized, callous and whimsical, holding autocratic sway over lower, larger vassals like herself.

There followed a punishing stint of ricochet work, where Frances let the baby cry while she comforted Lorna; let Lorna shriek while she soothed the baby; put Lorna down for her nap and was called back three times before she gave up and let her follow her destructively around; bathed the baby after he had sprayed himself, Lorna and the bathroom with urine during the nappy changing process; sat on the closed lavatory seat and fed the baby while Lorna chattered in the bath which she had demanded in the wake of the baby's bath.

She stared at Lorna's slim silver body, exquisite in the water, graceful as a Renaissance statuette.

'Shall we see if you'd like a little nap after your bath?' she suggested hopelessly, for only if Lorna rested would she be able to rest, and then only if Matthew was asleep or at least not ready for a feed.

'No,' said Lorna, off-hand but firm.

'Oh thank God,' said Frances as she heard the car door slam outside. Jonathan was back. It was like the arrival of the cavalry. She wrapped Lorna in a towel and they scrambled downstairs. Jonathan stood puffing on the doormat. Outside was a mid-afternoon twilight, the rain as thick as turf and drenching so that it seemed to leave no room for air between its stalks.

'You're wet, Daddy,' said Lorna, fascinated.

'There were lumps of ice coming down like tennis balls,' he marvelled.

'Here, have this towel,' said Frances, and Lorna span off naked as a sprite from its folds to dance among the chairs and tables while thunder crashed in the sky with the cumbersomeness of heavy furniture falling down uncarpeted stairs.

'*S'il vous plaît*,' said Frances to Jonathan, '*Dancez, jouez avec le petit diable, cette fille. Il faut que je* get Matthew down for a nap, she just wouldn't let me. *Je suis tellement* shattered.'

'Mummymummymummy,' Lorna chanted as she caught some inkling of this, but Jonathan threw the towel over her and they started to play ghosts.

'My little fat boy,' she whispered at last, squeezing his strong thighs. '*Hey*, fatty boomboom, *sweet* sugar dumpling. It's not fair, is it? I'm never alone with you. You're getting the rough end of the stick just now, aren't you.'

She punctuated this speech with growling kisses, and his hands and feet waved like warm pink roses. She sat him up and stroked the fine duck tail of hair on his baby bull neck. Whenever she tried to fix his essence, he wriggled off into mixed metaphor. And so she clapped his cloud cheeks and revelled in his nest of smiles; she blew raspberries into the crease of his neck and onto his astounded hardening stomach, forcing lion-deep chuckles from him.

She was dismayed at how she had to treat him like some sort of fancy man to spare her daughter's feelings, affecting nonchalance when Lorna was around. She would fall on him for a quick mad embrace if the little girl left the room for a moment, only to spring apart guiltily at the sound of the returning Start-rites.

The serrated teeth of remorse bit into her. In late pregnancy she had been so sandbagged that she had had barely enough energy to crawl through the day, let alone reciprocate Lorna's incandescent two-year-old passion.

'She thought I'd come back to her as before once the baby arrived,' she said aloud. 'But I haven't.'

The baby was making the wrangling noise which led to unconsciousness. Then he fell asleep like a door closing. She carried him carefully to his basket, a limp solid parcel against her bosom, the lashes long and wet on his cheeks, lower lip out in a soft semicircle. She put him down and he lay, limbs thrown wide, spatchcocked.

After the holiday, Jonathan would be back at the office with his broad quiet desk and filter coffee while she, she would have to submit to a fate worse than death, drudging round the flat to Lorna's screams and the baby's regurgitations and her own sore eyes and body aching to the throb of next door's Heavy Metal.

The trouble with prolonged sleep deprivation was, that it produced the same coarsening side effects as alcoholism. She was rotten with self-pity, swarming with irritability and despair.

When she heard Jonathan's step on the stairs, she realized that he must have coaxed Lorna to sleep at last.

She looked forward to his face, but when he came into the room and she opened her mouth to speak, all that came out were toads and vipers.

'I'm smashed up,' she said. 'I'm never alone. The baby guzzles me and Lorna eats me up. I can't ever go out because I've always got to be there for the children, but you flit in and out like a humming bird. You need me to be always there, to peck at and pull at and answer the door. I even have to feed the cat.'

'I take them out for a walk on Sunday afternoons,' he protested.

'But it's like a favour, and it's only a couple of hours, and I can't use the time to read, I always have to change the sheets or make a meatloaf.'

'For pity's sake. I'm tired too.'

'Sorry,' she muttered. 'Sorry. Sorry. But I don't feel like me any more. I've turned into some sort of oven.'

They lay on the bed and held each other.

'Did you know what Hardy called *Jude the Obscure* to begin with?' he whispered in her ear. '*The Simpletons*. And the Bishop of Wakefield burnt it on a bonfire when it was published.'

'You've been reading!' said Frances accusingly. '*When* did you read!'

'I just pulled in by the side of the road for five minutes. Only for five minutes. It's such a good book. I'd completely forgotten that Jude had three children.'

'*Three?*' said Frances. 'Are you sure?'

'Don't you remember Jude's little boy who comes back from Australia?' said Jonathan. 'Don't you remember little Father Time?'

'Yes,' said Frances. 'Something very nasty happens to him, doesn't it?'

She took the book and flicked through until she reached the page where little Time and his siblings are discovered by their mother hanging from a hook inside a cupboard door, the note at their feet reading, 'Done because we are too menny.'

'What a wicked old man Hardy was!' she said, incredulous. 'How *dare* he!' She started to cry.

'You're too close to them,' murmured Jonathan. 'You should cut off from them a bit.'

'How *can* I?' sniffed Frances. '*Somebody*'s got to be devoted to them. And it's not going to be you because you know I'll do it for you.'

'They're yours, though, aren't they, because of that,' said Jonathan. 'They'll love you best.'

'They're *not* mine. They belong to themselves. But I'm not allowed to belong to *my* self any more.'

'It's not easy for me either.'

'I know it isn't, sweetheart. But at least you're still allowed to be your own man.'

They fell on each other's necks and mingled maudlin tears.

'It's so awful,' sniffed Frances. 'We may never have another.'

They fell asleep.

When they woke, the landscape was quite different. Not only had the rain stopped, but it had rinsed the air free of oppression. Drops of water hung like lively glass on every leaf and blade. On their way down to the beach, the path was hedged with wet hawthorn, the fiercely spiked branches glittering with green-white flowers.

The late sun was surprisingly strong. It turned the distant moving strokes of the waves to gold bars, and dried salt patterns onto the semi-precious stones which littered the shore. As Frances unbuckled Lorna's sandals, she pointed out to her translucent pieces of chrysoprase and rose quartz in amongst the more ordinary egg-shaped pebbles. Then she kicked off her own shoes and walked wincingly to the water's edge. The sea was casting lacy white shawls onto the stones, and drawing them back with a sigh.

She looked behind her and saw Lorna building a pile of pebbles while Jonathan made the baby more comfortable in his pushchair. A little way ahead was a dinghy, and she could see the flickering gold veins on its white shell thrown up by the sun through moving seawater, and the man standing in it stripped to the waist. She walked towards it, then past it, and as she walked on, she looked out to sea and was aware of her eyeballs making internal adjustments to the new distance which was being demanded of them, as though they had forgotten how to focus on a long view. She felt an excited bubble of pleasure expanding her ribcage, so that she had to take little sighs of breath, warm and fresh and salted, and prevent herself from laughing aloud.

After some while she reached the far end of the beach. Slowly she wheeled, like a hero on the cusp of anagnorisis, narrowing her eyes to make out the little group round the pushchair. Of course it was satisfying and delightful to see Jonathan – she supposed it *was* Jonathan? – lying with the fat mild baby on his stomach while their slender elf of a daughter skipped around him. It was part of it. But not the point of it. The concentrated delight was there to start with. She had not needed babies and their pleased-to-be-alive-ness to tell her this.

She started to walk back, this time higher up the beach in the shade of cliffs which held prehistoric snails and traces of dinosaur. I've done it, she thought, and I'm still alive. She took her time, dawdling with deliberate pleasure, as though she were carrying a full glass of milk and might not spill a drop.

'I thought you'd done a Sergeant Troy,' said Jonathan. 'Disappeared out to sea and abandoned us.'

'Would I do a thing like that,' she said, and kissed him lightly beside his mouth.

Matthew reached up from his arms and tugged her hair.

'When I saw you over there by the rock pools you looked just as you used to,' said Jonathan. 'Just the same girl.'

'I am not just as I was, however,' said Frances. 'I am no longer the same girl.'

The sky, which had been growing more dramatic by the minute, was now a florid stagey empyrean, the sea a soundless blaze beneath it. Frances glanced at the baby, and saw how the sun made an electric fleece of the down on his head. She touched it lightly with the flat of her hand as though it might burn her.

'Isn't it mind-boggling,' said Jonathan. 'Isn't it impossible to take in that when we were last on this beach, these two were thin air. Or less. They're so solid now that I almost can't believe there was a time before them, and it's only been a couple of years.'

'What?' said Lorna. '*What* did you say?'

'Daddy was just commenting on the mystery of human existence,' said Frances, scooping her up and letting her perch on her hip. She felt the internal chassis, her skeleton and musculature, adjust to the extra weight with practised efficiency. To think, she marvelled routinely, to think that this great heavy child grew in the centre of my body. But the surprise of the idea had started to grow blunt, worn down by its own regular self-contemplation.

'Look, Lorna,' she said. 'Do you see how the sun is making our faces orange?'

In the flood of flame-coloured light their flesh turned to coral.

The Immaculate Bridegroom

Dawn climbed smiling up from her warm white dream, magnolia petal slippers whispering in the cathedral hush beneath wild silk underskirts, enormously hooped, and bud-studded gypsophila like a mystic cloud of gnats: then reached the top, real life again, and felt her face drop, along with her heart, and stomach, and the corners of her mouth.

'It's not fair,' she said. She turned her head on the pillow and stared at the wallpaper. This was a tangled but repetitious pattern of tiny briar roses she had seized on for her boudoir twenty years ago, a rare choice allowed by her parents at the onset of adolescence, and never regretted.

'What's wrong, darling?' said her mother, Sylvia, appearing with the tea.

'Oh, the usual,' grunted Dawn, heaving herself up and jutting out her underlip like a thwarted baby. 'I'm fed up. I want everything to be different.'

'It does seem so unfair,' tutted Sylvia.

'It is,' Dawn agreed.

'Sometimes I curse Roger,' said Sylvia.

Dawn gave a soft scream and rounded on her.

'I *told* you, Mum!' she hissed. 'If you mention his name again, I'll.'

'Sorry dear,' said Sylvia. 'I can't help thinking of all those years.'

'Well, *don't*,' said Dawn, heaving herself out of bed and over to the dressing table. She scowled into its triple mirror, her profile aping the hard-nosed sullenness of a Quattrocento Gonzaga.

'Who knows what might turn up,' said her mother hopelessly.

'Nothing ever does, though, turn up, does it,' said Dawn in injured tones. 'I'll tell you what, Mum, I don't see why the likes of Sandra Bailey who was never anything special, and great fat legs, why she should have her big day and not me.'

'It does seem cruel,' Sylvia agreed. 'We'd manage it much better than Sandra Bailey and her mother.'

'I don't see why I should be done out of it.'

'No, *I* don't see why you should be done out of it.'

'The most important day of my life.'

'I *don't* see why,' said Sylvia. 'And I'm being done out of it too, your big day. The bride's mother. It's obviously completely unfair.'

Dawn got up and started prowling round the bedroom, abstractedly brushing her hair, which crackled with static under the bristles.

'You're a modern girl,' said her mother admiringly. 'You don't have to put up with things.'

'No,' said Dawn. 'I don't.'

'Don't make the mistakes I did,' said Sylvia. 'Too passive. Putting up with things.'

'You're absolutely right, Mum!' said Dawn, pausing by
the Rossetti poster of Beata Beatrix, taut with the bright-
eyed rapture of one to whom the truth has been revealed.
Then she sagged. 'But. Even so. It would be awfully
difficult . . .'

Sylvia leaned forward urgently across the tea tray.

'Nothing worth having's ever easy, Dawn,' she enunci-
ated.

'So you think . . . ?'

'Follow your heart's desire.'

'You're right!' breathed Dawn. 'Oh, Mum. I will!'

Dawn's father Harry was less than delighted at her news.

'Do you know what weddings cost?' he grunted. '*Do*
you?'

'Oh you old killjoy,' Sylvia twitted him.

'Anyway, when did Roger decide to do the decent
thing?' said Harry. 'First I've heard of it. Thought he
disappeared off the scene years ago.'

'It's not Roger,' said Dawn, pink-cheeked, her eyes
starting to brim.

'Then who the hell is it?' said Harry.

'Trust you to be difficult,' snapped Sylvia. 'Can't you see
you're upsetting the girl, Harry? Marriages are made in
Heaven. Killjoy. You have to *work* at a marriage. You
wouldn't deny that, I suppose!' She paused for a bitter
laugh. 'You wouldn't deny I've had to work at our
marriage like some poor devil of a pit pony while you've
suited yourself. No. You wouldn't have the nerve!'

'What?' said Harry.

'Come on, darling,' said Sylvia. 'Let's ring your aunts.

Your cousins. Tell them the good news. He's thrilled for you really, he just needs time to get used to the idea.'

Once Dawn had found two friends willing to act as bridesmaids, they convened in a winebar to chew over past weddings and plan this one.

'Amethysts like little mauve raindrops,' sighed Milly. 'A sort of pomander affair made of stephanotis and love-in-a-mist looped round her wrist on a ribbon. You can imagine. With *her* hair.'

'Sort of fluffy, her hair,' said Dawn thoughtfully.

'Yes, not exactly everyday hair,' said Milly. 'But perfect under tulle, that shade of yellow, like a baby chick. Oh, I do love weddings! They're my absolute favourite thing.'

Milly sat on the other side of the corridor from Dawn at work. Dawn hadn't known her for very long but she seemed quite kind and posh and would know what's what. Also, while she wasn't risibly spotty or funny looking, neither was she particularly pretty, which was ideal. The same went for Christine on the looks front, though Dawn had known her much longer, since school-days.

'So tell us about him,' said Christine, draining her second glass and stuffing in a handful of dry roast. 'Mr Right. Where did you meet him?'

'Yes, we don't even know his name!' said Milly. 'So mysterious!'

'Rochester,' said Dawn.

'Rochester?' said Christine. 'What on earth were you doing in Rochester?'

'No,' said Dawn. 'That's his name. Mr Rochester.' She paused. 'Tony.'

'And is he tall, dark and handsome?' enquired Christine sharply.

'Yes,' said Dawn. 'At least, I think so.'

'I should hope so!' said Milly. 'That you do, I mean. That's all that matters, isn't it.'

'Yes,' said Dawn.

'Unlike Patrick,' said Christine violently, pouring herself another glass. 'He's a first-class shit.'

'Patrick's her boyfriend,' Dawn explained to Milly.

The talk turned to the unsatisfactory nature of modern men, the way they seemed to flit around now more than they ever used to, never building anything up, never tying themselves down, never amounting to much.

'They take eight or nine of your best years,' snarled Christine. 'Keep you hanging on and hanging on, then they bugger off when crunch time comes.'

'Patrick's not about to do that, is he?' asked Dawn shrewdly.

'Your Roger was classic, though,' said Christine, intercutting. 'Leaving you high and dry at thirty-three. Fantastic.'

They looked at each other with dislike.

'But Tony's not like that,' said Milly, brightly, at last. 'Hopefully.'

'What does Tony do?' asked Christine.

'He works in the world of finance,' said Dawn. There was a pause. '*High* finance,' she added softly.

'And how did he propose?' asked Christine in spite of herself.

'It wasn't in so many words,' said Dawn, her eyes shining out at the middle distance. 'It was more we became aware. Both of us. That we'd somehow found our other half. I feel so at home with him that it's almost like being on my own. We two are one.'

'So when can we meet him?' asked Christine. 'Your other half.'

'The thing is,' said Dawn, 'he has a very responsible job. He's rarely around.'

'Your time together is precious,' suggested Milly.

'Surely he relaxes sometimes,' said Christine.

'Well, he has his, his club,' said Dawn.

'What?' said Christine. 'Golf? How old is he?'

'He does it for his health,' said Dawn. She fiddled with her bracelet. 'He has a weak heart,' she added, with a sudden hard look.

After that, preparations for the wedding started in earnest. Sylvia bought a book on how to do it, packed with prescriptive nuptial etiquette and including a countdown list of which jobs needed doing when and by whom.

'It's good luck for you to see a sweep on the way to church,' she said distractedly. 'Or a grey horse. I don't know which would be more difficult to arrange. Which would you prefer, dear?'

'Milly's got an Edwardian sixpence for my shoe,' said Dawn with satisfaction.

'The bridegroom's function,' read Sylvia, suddenly anxious. 'He buys the ring. That's all right, you can have mine. Call it an heirloom. He provides the bride's mother's corsage, first checking the colour of her outfit to avoid colour clashes. I think I can manage that. Oh. He tips the verger.'

'What's a verger?' asked Dawn.

'It doesn't say,' said Sylvia. 'We'll have to find out.'

'Cooker hood. Nutcrackers. Step-ladder,' read Dawn, turning to the list of suggested wedding presents. 'Cream jug. Wok. Skillet. What's a skillet when it's at home?'

'I wouldn't include too many little things like the nutcrackers,' said Sylvia. 'Or the cream jug. People can be very mean. Specially relatives.'

'Music in church,' Dawn went on, flicking through the pages. She started to hum. 'I quite liked that one the Princess of Wales had at her wedding. You know, "I vow to thee my country".'

'That was a *real* wedding,' crooned Sylvia. 'Just like a fairytale. You can't take that away, you can't say it wasn't perfect. Nothing to do with what came after.'

'No,' agreed Dawn. 'It was above all that. And I liked the wedding in *The Sound of Music* too, just before the interval. Seven step-children, though. Quite a handful.'

'She was the sort who was good with children, though, wasn't she,' said Sylvia. 'She went on to do Mary Poppins.'

'The Arrival of the Queen of Sheba!' said Dawn. 'I'll have that. You remember, Mum, I did it for Grade V. *Dudda* dudda *dudda* dudda *dudda* dudda *dudda* dudda *da* da da da da da da da *da* dee *da* dee *da* dee *da* dee DUDDA dudda!' She ran out of breath and started laughing.

The invitations, spidered with soft silvery italics, took two days to address, owing to the invitees' complicated web of *mésalliances*, formal and otherwise, tearings asunder, third-time-roundings, and only the occasional straightforward nuclear smugness to speed things up.

'You see, look,' said Sylvia. 'Your cousin Bridget, she was born Bridget Riley, but she married George Filmer.'

'George Filmer!' snorted Harry.

'We all make mistakes,' said Sylvia. 'So they'd have been Mr and Mrs George Filmer, and if he'd died she'd still be Mrs George Filmer. But she divorced, didn't she, after the Stanley knife incident, so then she was Mrs Bridget Filmer. Not Riley again, mark you, not the name she was born with.'

'Her father's name,' said Harry. 'Now he *was* a bugger. No wonder she didn't want *his* name back.'

'But then she married again, Robert Billington, God rest his soul. So now she's Mrs Robert Billington, even though poor Bob's passed away.'

'She did all right out of that, didn't she,' said Harry. 'She's a powerful woman now. All that life insurance. No one ever mentioned seeing a Stanley knife, did they, on the scene, when Bob's body was found?'

'Harry,' said Sylvia. 'I'm warning you. One crack like that at the reception and I'll.'

'Do we *have* to have cousin Bridget?' said Dawn pensively.

'Yes,' said Sylvia. 'She's your flesh and blood. Unfortunately.'

'Mrs Dawn Rochester,' smiled Dawn.

'No,' said Harry. 'Mrs Tony Rochester. You'd have to give him the push before you could call yourself Dawn again.'

'Oh, yes,' said Dawn, looking mildly confused. 'So I would.'

There was no getting round it, said Sylvia, they would have to see the vicar. They couldn't leave it any longer, putting it off and putting it off. She had hinted at the possibility of a putative future hiccup on the phone and he had said, well, he'd have to see, but most things were not insurmountable these days, always allowing for the bishop.

Once in his front room, mother and daughter found themselves crouching forward, chins thrust out sincerely, faces reddened by the horrible realization that what they wanted might not be allowed to happen.

'The thing is, Vicar,' said Sylvia, 'Dawn's fiancé has a very responsible job. He's never there.'

'My goodness me,' said the rector. He searched their faces for existential satire, but saw nothing like that beneath the sweat of their embarrassment.

'He's in the world of finance,' Dawn chipped in.

'So we were wondering,' said Sylvia in a rush, 'if by any remote chance he wasn't able to be there on the day, and we're ninety-nine-point-nine per cent sure he *will* be of course, well, in that event perhaps we could arrange a proxy.'

'A proxy?' said the rector, who had been expecting a double divorcee, say, or a bigamist, but not this.

'Do you remember Prince Arthur? Henry VII's eldest boy?' said Sylvia. 'Well, his father wanted a dynastic marriage with Spain, because the Tudors were new, not really supposed to be there, so he married little Arthur off to the Infanta, but the children were too young to marry really. So they sent a proxy over to Madrid, to stand in for the prince.'

Sylvia had an encyclopaedic knowledge of the various ins and outs of the British monarchy from the Plantagenets onward, acquired during forty-odd years of reading nothing much but Jean Plaidy and Anya Seton.

'On the wedding night,' she continued, 'the proxy touched the Infanta's naked shin with the heel of his bare foot, and that counted as a symbol of the,' she lowered her eyes modestly, 'the consummation of the marriage. So we were wondering, Vicar, if in the unlikely event that Dawn's intended was called away, on her big day I mean . . .'

'. . . by the world of finance . . .'

'. . . by the world of finance, yes, would a, a proxy be acceptable to you? Because the boy next door's quite willing to stand in. He's the sort who's naturally unpopular, so he'd do anything for you. We've known him years, he and Dawn used to play French skipping but she's never fancied him. In fact I think he's probably the other way if anything.'

'Oh he is,' said Dawn. 'It's a fact. He came out in January.'

'Oh?' said Sylvia. 'That's news to me.'

'It'd be news to his mother too,' said Dawn. 'He's doing it generation by generation, working back gradually. To the difficult ones. Personally, I wish him well.'

'Excuse me,' said the rector. 'May I interrupt at this point? Well, Sylvia. Well, Dawn. My turn now. I want to let you know where I stand *vis à vis* the horns of your dilemma. And that directly relates to my views on the Church of England.'

'Yes, Vicar,' said Sylvia. 'Dawn, sit up straight.'

'Strongly ecumenical though my sympathies are,' continued the rector, 'I cannot help but feel that the Church of England has a superior understanding of life's complexities. We are capable of responding to the changing needs of humanity, indeed to the passage of time itself. We shift. And we are proud to shift. When necessary. You know the story about the oak tree breaking and the reed bending? Well, that is what I love about the Church of England – its reediness. Dawn, are you listening?'

'Yes Vicar,' said Dawn, who had been thinking she ought to do her nails tonight, it was getting urgent.

'Now, Dawn, as I see it,' said the rector, 'you are a lamb newly returned to the fold.'

'What, like the prodigal son?' said Dawn, resentfully.

'She's been a good daughter,' said Sylvia. 'A model daughter.'

'I'm sure she has. So I take it you will both agree to come to church every Sunday until Dawn's wedding and at least every other Sunday for the next five years, by which time I hope you will both be as they say "hooked". On pain of annulment of the marriage if either of you default, I'm afraid.'

'They certainly squeeze their pound of flesh out of you these days, vicars,' said Sylvia. 'I'm sure it never used to be like that.'

She had baked a cake for seven hours at Mark 2, in a tin lined with double greaseproof and protected outside by a palisade of three thicknesses of newspaper tied with string. This cake and its two smaller companions had been cooled, painted with hot jam, cooled again, marzipanned, then given a bubble-free royal icing mantle on four consecutive evenings.

Now Sylvia attached a number two writing nozzle to the icing bag and started to inscribe in tiny cursive script, 'Let me not to the marriage of true minds.'

'It's quite long,' said Dawn anxiously. 'Are you sure you'll get it all on?'

'Fourteen lines,' said Sylvia. 'I've done it before.'

'It's just I'd hate to lose the last couplet,' fussed Dawn.

'Only one *d* in impediment,' clucked Sylvia. 'Blast. I hate that word.'

The night before, Dawn could not sleep. She sat in her little bedroom and looked round for what she imagined would be the last time at the miniature rose wallpaper, the herd of furry toys, Lizzie Siddal in a frizzy shroud of hair, the bookshelf freighted with flower fairies, Milly-Molly-Mandies and fantastical tales of princesses and boarding schools.

The trouble was, she acknowledged, she could not think what he looked like. She could imagine a looming shape in the doorway, a dark brown voice, a muscular thigh. But she could not envisage his face. After a while this bothered her so much that she called out to her mother, who was sitting up late with a fine black felt-tip stroking in a cross-bar on each Order of Service sheet in the line which read: *And did those feel in ancient times.*

'If I'm honest, Mum,' she sniffed, 'I'm not sure how well I really know him.'

'That's only natural, darling,' said Sylvia. 'You're not married yet.'

'But he seems sort of shadowy.'

'Plenty of time for the solid stuff after the wedding. Things *should* be dreamy before.'

'Am I doing the right thing, though?' wept Dawn. 'What if he turns out like Roger? Or Dad?'

'Listen Dawn,' said Sylvia sharply. 'He's an altogether different class of man. He won't.'

'But am I really in love?' she wailed.

'Of course you are!' snapped Sylvia. 'Pull yourself together. What do you want to do? Give the ring back? Call it all off? It's a bit late in the day for that, you know.'

'I know,' said Dawn, trumpeting into a tissue. 'Sorry, Mum. It didn't seem quite real for a minute there. Just nerves.'

Four hours of the early part of the morning had been allowed for the preparation of the bride, and that allowance had not proved excessive. Dawn's colour had been rising steadily since she woke up; she was now very pink indeed under her heated rollers and had almost stopped breathing.

'I think I've got a temperature,' she puffed.

'Excitement,' said Milly knowledgeably, freezing her nail varnish with a fixative spray. 'Don't worry, I've got some green make-up on me. I've done this before. You'll look like an arum lily by the time I've finished with you.'

117

Sylvia was peeling the price tag from the sole of the bride's gentian satin courts.

'Something blue, I imagine *they're* supposed to be,' Christine sniffed.

'A bit distracting for the congregation,' said Sylvia. 'While the bride kneels for her vows, £39.99 cast up at them. They *are* blue, Christine, no "supposed" about it.'

'Don't forget to step out of the house on your right foot when you leave for church,' said Milly. 'Or it's bad luck forever.'

'Oh dear,' said Dawn. 'There's such a lot to remember.'

Milly and Christine, sugar-pink caryatids in sashed and sprigged Swiss lawn, helped Dawn, by now gasping for air like a fish, into the wedding dress. It was a square-necked seersucker gown with leg-o'-mutton sleeves and a hundred and eighty-two hand-covered buttons.

'Ooooh,' went the women, with the sigh that people make as fireworks fade.

When Dawn and her father arrived at the church, the rector hurried forward to meet them with a long face.

'I'm afraid I have something of a disappointment for you, my dear,' he said to Dawn.

She recoiled in a rustle of puckered silk.

'You promised,' she hissed, a furious swan on the path. 'You promised!'

'Never fear,' said the rector hurriedly, with a lopsided smile. 'What I was going to say was, it looks as though our gallant proxy may be called on after all.'

Then Dawn put a hand to her thumping heart and smiled, while Harry turned and waved at the limousine parked by the lych gate. Out jumped the boy-next-door, spruce and shy. They shooed him into the church before them, waited a moment and then, at a sign from the rector, the opening chords of the Arrival of the Queen of Sheba cascaded down and they went slowly in.

Just as a camcorder may cause offence during a wedding ceremony, so may an authorial presence. Imagination must supply the dog-rose blushes of the bride beneath her clouding of organdie tulle, the satin slippers moving at the hem of her dress like blue-nosed mice, and the soaring and crashing of the organ music.

Some guests could not help but notice, however, that what with the bride's family seated shoulder to shoulder in the left-hand pews and only the mother of the boy-next-door on the right, there was something of an imbalance. The church had lolled like a clumsily ballasted ship.

There was some comment on this at the reception afterwards.

'Bit of a one-sided wedding,' said an aunt from Birkenhead.

'Bit of a one-horse affair all round,' replied Mrs Robert Billington. 'Not even a sit-down meal.'

'I mean, did you notice,' persisted the aunt. 'Our side of the church was packed, but on the other side nobody but the next-door neighbour.'

'Ironic, really, after all these years, to end up with the boy-next-door,' sniffed Mrs Billington.

'Though someone was telling me he was only a stand-in,' puzzled the aunt.

'A stand-in?' said Mrs Billington. 'A stand-in for what?'

'That's what I said,' the aunt agreed. She shrugged.

'Dawn makes a lovely bride, though, doesn't she. Bless her.'

The bride's father's speech concentrated on anecdotes relating to his daughter's tantrums, teenage skin complaints, and disastrous sexual escapades, on her tendency to treat money like water and to cry at the drop of a hat.

'Tony had better tread carefully, that's all I can say!' he finished. 'I must admit, though, from what I've seen, he's not exactly keen to throw his weight around. It's a shame he couldn't be here with us today – these high fliers – but rest assured everyone, he will be there to meet Dawn off the plane at the honeymoon destination. More than that I'm not allowed to divulge.'

Then Dawn ran whooping through an archway of hands and a shower of rice, off out to the car and away. Sylvia stood and cried.

'There, there,' said Harry. 'He'll take good care of her.'

And he obviously did. She came back brown as a Sunday roast – radiant! It was a shame he'd had to carry on from St Lucia but it would have been foolish not to fly on to the Philippines to clinch the deal he'd been working on at the time of their wedding, and Dawn was quite happy about that.

'I'm not worried,' she said to Milly and Christine at their post-honeymoon get-together to view the wedding photographs. 'He can look after himself.'

The story should end here, happily ever after so to speak; unfortunately it is necessary to add a coda.

Such serenity, such newly wed insouciance, threw the blow, when it fell, into cruelly sharp relief. News of Tony's

demise on foreign shores, a massive coronary at a vital
convention, tragic though it undoubtedly was, and of
course untimely, apparently trailed clouds of fiscal glory.
His actions that day, just before the fatal stoppage, had
saved the livelihoods of thousands of shareholders, Dawn
told them (though it had left her no better off than before
since, oddly enough, he had died without leaving a bean).
She mopped her eyes and blew her nose with subdued
grace.

Widowhood had conferred on Dawn an unexpected
gravitas. It soon became apparent that she was not after all
utterly bereft. This was discovered following the harrow-
ing news of Tony's decease, when she hinted that their all-
too-brief honeymoon had borne fruit.

Tony had not died without issue, it seemed, or, at least,
not exactly. Dawn grew bulkier by the week and devel-
oped a sleepy smile. There was some comfort in this
situation, friends and relatives remarked; she would have
someone to cherish. It would be company for her. And if
the child were a boy – as indeed eventually proved to be
the case – then his father's name, as well as his memory,
would live on.

Caput Apri

It was Boxing Day and I must say I was quite glad to get out of the house. Another batch of in-laws had arrived that morning, and after a couple of hours of being chirpy I was actually pleased to find I'd forgotten the cranberries.

'I won't be a moment,' I promised. 'I'll just shoot down to Cullen's.'

It was lovely outside, frosty and sparkling, white ducks swimming on the village pond and so on. This was all very nice and I started to feel more cheerful. Along past the church I looked up and saw red berries and dark green holly leaves against the blue sky.

'Like a child's painting, isn't it,' said a voice at my shoulder.

You can always trust Yvonne Maitland to come out with something like that. How would one describe her? She's not exactly eccentric but on the other hand she's what my son would call, slightly off the wall. A wee bit arty. I was relieved to see Patricia Baron coming towards us. Salt of the earth, Patricia. On the same wavelength.

We chatted for a while about trees shedding needles and

that sort of thing. Patricia was planning a picnic for her
husband to take to the races, a flask of game soup, a manly
steak sandwich, she didn't seem overjoyed.

'Aren't you going?' I asked.

'Oh no,' she sniffed. 'Client entertainment. No *wives*.'
Her husband's with Bonner Kelman and Witt so she
hardly ever sees him.

'Tough cheddar,' I said sympathetically. My husband's
with Parringdon Knebworthy so I know the score.

'These City gents,' said Yvonne unexpectedly. She'd
been watching us with her head on one side like a beady
little robin. 'Let's have a drink,' she suggested. 'They're
doing mulled wine at the White Horse, there's a log fire,
we'll only be ten minutes.'

I saw Patricia hesitate. I was about to say no, surprised
myself by barking out a Yes, and then Patricia caved in too.

We managed to bag a table by the fire and Yvonne
organized the wine, which went straight to our heads in a
very Christmassy way.

'This is fun,' said Patricia. 'If Malcolm could see me
now.'

'I sometimes think,' said Yvonne, and stopped. She
looked at us with an odd sort of expression. 'Let me tell
you a story,' she said. 'It's all true, though I don't expect
you'll believe me.'

I was quite happy to sit back holding my warm glass,
and I could see Patricia felt the same, more than happy to
let her chat away while we relaxed.

She started to tell the story, and I must say she told it
very well, all the voices and actions and so forth. It was

actually quite riveting. We soon forgot about the time completely.

Everard Ravenscroft possessed that blend of physical energy and emotional ruthlessness which is often called charisma (said Yvonne, her eyes in the middle distance, her mouth stained with hot wine). He flashed his sarcastic phrases like scissors around his family's ears, keeping them cowed and resentful. A fit fat barrister, he felt the cruelty was warranted, even salutary, a father's way of keeping them up to scratch.

One Christmas Day some years ago, Everard was sitting at the head of the dining table carving a fine varnished turkey watched by his wife Marion, who had cooked the bird, his son Charlie (shaking slightly as a result of substances ingested at a party attended the previous night), his permanently sulky adolescent daughter Natasha, and his youngest child, five-year-old Lucy.

'Good old turkey. Year in year out,' said Everard, addressing his wife. 'Sometimes, though, my dear, I must say I long to escape its flavourless clutches. Those mounds of bland flesh languishing for days afterwards.'

'You didn't like the spiced beef the year I did it,' she said.

'No no. No more I did. It was quite repellently salty,' said Everard amiably. 'But perhaps another year we might have, let's see, a goose stuffed with Gascon prunes? A fruited loin of pork? Or even – memento of college days, that special Saturday before Christmas – a boar's head with a sodding great lemon in its mouth?'

'How totally disgusting,' said vegetarian Natasha,

whose plate held a cheerless congregation of sprouts and potatoes. 'That makes me want to vomit.'

Her father narrowed his eyes dangerously at her and smiled his long thin smile. He had fierce light little eyes of arctic blue. The smile showed his teeth, which were all sharp and shipshape if rather yellow.

'*Caput apri defero*,' he boomed. '*Reddens laudes Domino*. The bore's heed in hande bringe I with garlans gay and rosemarie.'

Charlie closed his eyes involuntarily, as though caught in a high bitter wind.

'And do you know why us students used to sing a carol to the boar?' Everard continued, loud and remorseless. 'Because a long time ago, a *very* long time ago, a Queen's man was walking in the woods at Hinksey when a wild boar rushed out at him. Savage brute. Tusks to rip a horse up. Unluckily for him our man was carrying a copy of Aristotle's *Nicomachian Ethics* (which I feel you might read with some profit Natasha and you too Charlie in the not too distant future), and this he stuffed down the boar's throat, shouting GRAECUM EST.'

The table shuddered at the thunder of his voice.

'Then he cut off his head. The student cut off the boar's head, that is. Took it back to the college kitchen. And ever since.'

He stopped and surveyed the silent dinner table with satisfaction. Clubbing them into submission with some crashing great anecdote was one of his favourite techniques. Natasha stared at him, at the big short-necked head with its brutally turfy haircut, and envisioned it borne aloft on a pewter dish of herbs.

'That's what's wrong with modern life,' continued Everard. 'It's tame. It's bland. It's not done to mention that the secret of success is a matter of attack, of combative flair, that the law of the jungle is not just an empty expression.'

'Darling,' said Marion plaintively. 'It *is* Christmas.'

After the meal they all trooped off to the sitting room and dropped pensively into various armchairs.

'Can we open our presents?' said Lucy. She had truffled out every package with her name on it from the mound of parcels beneath the tree.

'Wait,' said Marion. 'Just wait till I've poured the coffee, and we'll all open them together.'

'I suppose I'd better fetch your present, hadn't I,' said Everard. 'Where's the sellotape etcetera?'

'Cardboard box on the landing,' said Marion tonelessly. Everard groaned and set off, mock-lugubrious.

In his absence, Natasha opened her present, purchased by her mother, paid for by her father, a jar of precious Pompeian massage oil as requested, and gloated over it in a sultry cloud of narcissism. She and Charlie had jointly bought their mother a reversible velvet scarf and their father a silver money clip.

'You didn't get me the Barbie disco set!' wailed Lucy. 'I *told* you to get the Barbie disco set! I hate you!'

'I did,' said Marion hurriedly. 'I *did*, darling. *Look*, darling. What's this?'

'That's the Barbie aerobic studio. I don't want that! I hate *that*! Oh!'

Lucy gave a shriek of grief and ran screaming from the room, remembering however, even in the extremity of emotion, to give a wide berth to her father as he re-entered with a hastily wrapped package.

'Happy Christmas,' he smiled, and Marion took the proffered parcel with a look of sullen fright. 'That child.'

'It's her age,' she said stiffly. 'Here's yours.' And she wheeled out an elaborate glittering construct from behind the piano.

'My goodness,' said Everard smugly. 'I wonder what this can be.'

'It took her hours to wrap,' Natasha accused him. 'She was crackling away all through *Where Eagles Dare.*'

'My goodness,' said Everard again, knee-deep in shimmering wrappings, staring at a bag of top-notch golf clubs.

'I can change them,' Marion said. 'They said if I brought them back within twenty-one days.'

'Just what I wanted,' he said, and she winced as he landed a display kiss on her jaw.

Then she turned to her own parcel with the air of a bomb disposal expert confronted with an unfamiliar landmine.

'I hope it fits,' said Everard pleasantly, as she shook out the huge shroud-white nightdress, with its elasticated sleeves and high-necked goffered frill.

'Very practical,' gasped Marion.

'That frill's a bit like the bits on lamb cutlets,' said Charlie. 'Isn't it.'

'Mutton dressed as lamb!' laughed Marion, and ran sobbing into the Christmas tree. There was a soft gradual tinkling and rustling crash as one fell on top of the other.

After she had disentangled herself and struggled from the room covered in lametta, there was an awkward silence.

Then, 'She might have electrocuted herself on those lights,' commented Everard. 'Ridiculous.'

'Oh, dad,' said Natasha. 'You are beastly.'

'Oh, I'm such a villain,' said Everard. 'Such a wicked patriarch. It's hard, Charlie. You'll find it hard too with your excellent education. We're the current trendy target for attack, purely because we have the misfortune to be middle class and male. I'm afraid you'll find everyone hates you before you've even opened your mouth.'

'Too right,' muttered Natasha, and followed her mother upstairs.

'What a monstrous regiment, eh,' observed Everard, selecting a virgin niblick and slicing the air with relish.

Charlie scowled at his father's profile. He wished he could punch him on his aquiline nose. In fact he would quite like to kill him, he noticed, raising a mental eyebrow. He quivered with fatigue, hunched his shoulders up round his ears, thrust his hands into his pockets.

As his left hand closed involuntarily around the powdery matt tablet, he remembered the Discobiscuit. It had cost him fifteen pounds last night, cheap at the price if it was the real thing, though he strongly suspected it wasn't. Nobody seemed to have seen or heard of the dealer before, and when Charlie, mindful of stories about ground lightbulb glass, had tried questions about the provenance of what he was being offered he had been told to take it or leave it, but less politely.

With a chilly trickle of excitement, he now slid the Discobiscuit, unseen, into his father's coffee, where it fizzed gently for a moment or two. Then, mumbling an excuse, he left the room.

Some half-hour later, Lucy pattered downstairs to watch *Mary Poppins*. She stopped outside the sitting room when she heard the noises – vigorous snufflings and gruntings mixed with explosive gutturals. When she peeped around the door, her nose almost touched a flaring fleshy rosette, the open-nostrilled end to the wedge-like snout fronting the boar.

Its little eyes, gleaming with irritability and ill will, stared at her consideringly.

How could this be? You may well ask. The last wild boar in Britain was hunted to oblivion late in the eighteenth century. But butchers now will pay starry sums for meat from the hybrid marcassins sired by ex-zoo boars, housed in secure buildings under the Dangerous Animals Act: so perhaps this one was an escapee.

Perhaps.

Lucy's mouth opened to let out a thin high scream. She turned to run towards the stairs, and the boar, shrieking just as loudly, gave chase. When the child tripped, the boar thundered past her, its cloven trotters clipping the polished parquet flooring; and it turned its head slightly, dipped it down, *en passant*, to allow one eight-inch tusk to rip through a sleeve into her upper arm.

Suddenly silent, Lucy scrambled to her feet while the boar wheeled, cumbersome as a leather suitcase, at the end of the hall. Then she shot off back up to her mother's room, clutching her dripping arm, while the beast stood at the foot of the stairs squealing with frustration.

When Marion saw her bleeding child step towards her, she grew uncharacteristically fleet and efficient, calm as a lizard, while her heart beat a tattoo.

A cursory examination of the First Aid box showed only little strips of plaster, not the bandages needed to bind shut the flap of gashed flesh. She cast around for clean white linen, seized on the new nightdress as ideal, and tore off a long strip from central hem to yoke. This she bound tightly round Lucy's arm, and watched the white of the makeshift bandage turn seepingly to scarlet while she dialled for an ambulance.

Natasha appeared at the bedroom door, and Charlie beside her. They both looked terrified.

'There's some sort of enormous pig,' said Natasha. 'Standing at the bottom of the stairs. Mum. Covered in bristles like a doormat.'

'Ah,' said Marion with unnatural calm. 'So that's what happened to Lucy's arm.'

When they saw their little sister, white as the Ace of Diamonds, Natasha gave a moan of distress while Charlie burst into tears.

'For goodness' sake, Charlie,' said Marion fiercely. 'Don't frighten her. Don't make things worse. There, there. It's all right, darling.'

Lucy's eyelids were flickering and she looked ready to faint. Charlie gave a sob. They could hear the animal's screams rising up the stairwell.

Marion placed the child against a bank of pillows.

'Where's your father?' she enquired of Natasha and Charlie.

'Haven't seen him,' said Natasha.

'Last time I saw him he was, um, drinking coffee in the front room,' sniffed Charlie.

Marion's mouth folded into a lipless pleat and she set off for the stairs.

'Everard! Everard!' she yelled, then stopped abruptly, half-way down, as her eyes met those of the boar. They stared at each other in mutual recognition. Marion's jaw dropped open like a nutcracker. The boar, fixing her with its tiny murderous eye, started scrabbling and shrieking again, frantic to climb the stairs. Marion clutched at her neck and lurched back to the bedroom.

'Everard,' she said in a clothy voice. 'It's Everard.'

'Oh Mum,' said Natasha. 'Is he hurt?'

'No,' said Marion. 'You don't understand. It's Everard.'

'You said,' said Natasha gently. 'But is he *hurt*?'

Charlie cleared his throat and wiped his eyes.

'She means the hairy pig is Dad,' he said, adding, 'It's all my fault.'

'What are you talking about?' said Marion. 'Come on. Tell me.'

'I put something in his coffee,' said Charlie.

'Something? What something?' said Natasha. 'Some sort of drug?'

'Yes,' said Charlie.

'Drugs?' said Marion. 'You?'

'It isn't supposed to do this,' said Charlie helplessly. 'I mean, when you hallucinate, you might think you've turned into a wild boar. But you don't actually do it.'

'So *he* took the drug but he's forcing *us* to do the hallucinating,' said Natasha. 'I see. Typical.'

She went out of the room to look again.

'He's smashing up those chairs you restored, Mum. You

know, those ones you did in the upholstery class,' she called.

'We'll have to go downstairs,' said Marion, joining her at the banisters. 'If we're going to get Lucy to the ambulance when it arrives.'

Charlie slid in between them.

'She's gone to sleep,' he said. 'Or passed out. You sit with her, mother. We'll deal with, er, the animal.'

'Be careful,' said Marion. 'I don't want another of you needing stitches.'

'We'll be careful,' said Charlie. 'But you must stay in the room with Lucy. Keep her safe.'

Once Marion was out of the way Charlie started taking his father's weightier law books down from their shelves on the landing.

'Come on, Tasha,' he said. 'Ammunition.'

When they had built a workmanlike wall of fifty-odd volumes on the half landing, they paused to consider the boar.

It stood about three feet high, with a long ferocious wedge of a head on a hefty paving slab of a body. Its savage-looking tusks, one now dark with blood, gave it the mythical look of a woodcut in a bestiary, and were obviously well suited to their traditional task of destroying farmland and rooting up vineyards.

'Right,' said Charlie, and hurled *Equity and the Law of Trusts* straight at its head. He hit it in the eye and was rewarded with a bellow of fury.

'That's for sending me back to school when I said I'd kill myself,' he hissed.

Natasha took fire from her brother.

133

'And that's for never showing any interest in anything I've ever done,' she snarled, heaving *Private International Law* down the stairs.

'That's for telling me I've got no guts,' yelled Charlie. 'No staying power. No attack. I'll give you attack!' He threw book after book in a heavy rain.

'And that's for sneering at everything I've ever said,' cried Natasha, quite transported, white hot. 'Making me look stupid in front of my friends. Ignoring us all!'

The boar turned for a moment, half stunned by a blow to the temple from *The Law of Tort*'s sharp spine, groaning, swinging its long head from side to side; and in that moment, Charlie danced past it to the end of the hall, where the spotless golf trolley stood, and seized a No. 3 iron.

'Come on, then,' he said, baring his teeth. 'Let's see who's got guts now.'

'Charlie!' screamed Natasha as the boar, pawing the parquet, made ready to charge.

But Charlie was quick. He swung the club above his head as he ran, and brought it down with sickening accuracy so that the full force of the blow curled into the beast's throat.

They watched his strangulated coughing fit and cheered his gradual noisy keeling over.

'Knife,' hissed Natasha. 'I'll get the carving knife.'

She ran off to the kitchen, while Charlie watched him start to revive.

'Quick,' he shouted. 'Quick. Give it to me. The throat. It's the only soft bit, he's built like a tank everywhere else.'

Natasha walked back down the hall, holding the knife in

both hands, staring at the bristly space indicated by her brother. Then she blinked as Marion flew past them both, whitely wild as a madwoman by Fuseli, to cast herself upon the felled wild boar.

'You'll kill me first,' she declared to her children.

At this point the doorbell rang. In the ensuing confusion – nobody knew exactly when or how – the boar disappeared and there was Everard on the floor, groaning, a long cut running across his forehead. He was taken off to hospital in the same ambulance as his daughter Lucy, and like her was absolutely unable to tell the hospital staff how he had received his injuries. It was a mystery, was all he would say.

Since that strange Christmas Day, Everard has treated his first two children with real respect; and they, in turn, rein in their sense of damage done. As for his youngest daughter Lucy, he dotes on her, he knows the name of her best friend at school and of her second-best friend, he can tell you exactly how many teeth are in her head from day to day and precisely where she has got to in the Storychest scheme of things: but all this tenderness is painfully spiked, of course. In summer, when Lucy goes sleeveless, he winces at the scar on her arm, even though, sitting on his lap, she will laugh as she counts with her finger the seventeen stitch marks above his eyes. Then, of course, he is newly devoted to Marion, and the neighbours clack about the amount of time they spend together, about how often they are seen out walking, talking, dawdling around arm in arm for all the world as if Everard wasn't one of the top silks in the country.

Not any more, he isn't? No. Well. There you are.

Yvonne fell silent. A log shifted on the fire and I blinked at the little shower of sparks. It was dark outside. We'd been here for hours! Whatever would my mother-in-law say? She'd be phoning round the hospitals by now.

'Arm in arm,' said Patricia, a bit oddly I thought. 'Not much to ask, is it, you wouldn't have thought. Still.' She straightened her back, flashed me a cheery grin. 'Better be getting back to the ravening hordes!'

'They'll be baying for our blood by now,' I agreed.

Then I remembered something.

'Cranberries,' I said. 'Oh *sugar*.'

Creative Writing

'It's the ones who say "I want to know what *you* want to do" that you've got to watch,' explained Phyllis, doyenne of the evening class. 'When they say that, it means they've got no ideas.'

'But Quinn's excellent,' added Jill reassuringly. 'He's magic.'

They were addressing the latest addition to their group, Nadia, who, though dressed in lime-green mohair, fringed suede and lean diagonally zipped salopettes, looked rather at sea.

'If he knew anything worth knowing, he'd be published, wouldn't he?' snapped Karen. 'Not teaching people like us after work in a smelly library.' She was a doughty mixture of apathy and truculence, sitting through the lessons waiting to be ignited.

'Those who can, do,' said Phyllis sententiously. 'Those who can't, teach.' Like many of her profession, she was always quoting these words. She had taught Eng. Lit. until her retirement six years ago.

'Let's face it, none of us would be here if we were any good,' grumbled Karen.

'Oh thanks, Karen,' said Jill. 'That's the spirit. If you had any idea what I had to do and pay to be here tonight.'

Jill was married with several children, and these two hours on a Tuesday night were beadily noted and referred to by her home circle as 'Jill's Me-Time'.

'Sob sob,' said Karen. 'He's late. As usual.'

Nadia looked warily round the table. As well as Karen, Jill and Phyllis, she had also been introduced to Marion, Don and Jake. Marion was a housewife and mother in her middle fifties, recently shaken into attending this class by a sighting of her own imminent redundancy at home. Don was obviously extremely reticent, with hunched shoulders and inturning teeth, and had twitched in terror at her 'hello'. As for Jake, he was wearing an impressive leather jacket, ignoring everybody, reading a book called *Cultural Anarchy*. She wondered whether it was just by chance that he had taken the seat beside her.

There came a gust of cold air, the whip-whop of swing doors and then from round the corner of Modern Fiction appeared Quinn.

'Greetings,' he said, not mentioning his lateness, removing his tatty but fur-lined gloves. There came back a glad sycophantic mutter of welcome.

Quinn was a free spirit. Rumoured to have passed a decade in Left Bank cafés fossicking out palindromes with the likes of Perec and Queneau, he had also spent time in Barcelona, Vancouver, Manila and the Orkneys. Nobody knew how many wives he had had; his current mate was a tightrope walker, or perhaps that was just one of his metaphors. He never had any money but, extraordinarily, never mentioned this fact. Wherever he went people offered to buy him drinks. It was whispered that his feet were webbed.

'Let's start,' said Quinn. 'Now, last week we decided to give poetry a rest, to try a piece of prose instead. A story, even. I hope I warned you not to include more than four characters in any story; generally speaking, it's a recipe for disaster. And this story had to include if I remember rightly a mirror, three oxymorons and a reversal of fortune. How did we do? Karen, let's start with you.'

Karen cleared her throat and shuffled through the file in front of her.

'It's crap,' she shrugged. 'Still. Here you are. "I was sitting biting the end of my biro. I was trying to write a story but I couldn't come up with any ideas. I felt bored. I wanted to be doing something else. I felt like hoovering. Then I remembered my hair needed a wash. I still didn't have any ideas so I gave up and went to wash my hair." That's it,' she said, looking up scornfully.

'Ah,' said Quinn. 'This is metafiction, of course. How long did it take you?'

'I did it in the adverts during *Brookside*,' said Karen. 'It's crap, I know it's crap, you can't pretend it's not.'

'Well,' said Quinn thoughtfully, turning his eyes to the ceiling. 'I think you're being a little hard on yourself. But perhaps you're right. Did anyone have better luck than Karen with this exercise?'

Phyllis stuck her hand up and was soon reading aloud in a voice whose register quavered somewhere between grief and piety, a story of an elderly woman, happy at first in her garden with its shimmering trees, bees feasting on flowers, redolent, until the arrival of new neighbours, loutish, raucous, not heeding, shatters her world, causing her to feel disconsolate, despairing, desecrated. As she finished, she was obviously moved.

'A re-telling of *Paradise Lost*, in fact,' said Quinn, after a pause. 'Yes. And did I detect the influence of Rupert Brooke at several points here?'

'Certainly I am an admirer of his poetry,' said Phyllis, with a gracious nod of acknowledgement.

'Did you say what you wanted to say in this story?' said Quinn.

'I don't know,' said Phyllis equably. 'It depends on whether there's an intelligent reader.'

'Oh,' said Quinn. 'I suppose you might find one here. Yes. I wonder if you'd read that first paragraph again?'

'Outside,' she read, 'the rain was descending steadily, drumming upon the windowpanes. She sighed. She had risen that morning feeling more despondent than was her wont. She could barely summon the will to drag herself to the kettle.'

'Mmmm,' said Quinn. 'What do the rest of you think of this?'

'Basically,' said Jake. 'What you're saying there is, It was pissing down, she was pissed off.'

Phyllis bridled.

'Oh I see,' she snapped. 'So we've got to have piss everywhere, have we. "I looked out of the window and it was pissing down." I see.' She was blinking rapidly. 'I'm sorry, but I just call that sheer laziness. And ugliness.

There's nothing clever about swearing, you know. Anybody can say those words, the "f" word and so on, but some of us choose not to.'

'There's got to be a bit of bite somewhere, though, you must admit,' persisted Jake. 'Like Kafka said, a book must be the axe which smashes the frozen sea within us.'

'What do you mean,' said Nadia, speaking for the first time, 'a book must be an axe?'

'Keep your chopper to yourself, Jake,' said Jill, amiably enough.

'Jake,' said Quinn. 'May we hear your story, please.'

Jake read aloud a short disjunctive piece, laconic, flat, devoid of comment or adjectives or adverbs, involving an act of masturbation.

There was a silence once he had finished reading. People frowned seriously at the papers in front of them.

Quinn said, 'Thank you, Jake. What do the rest of you think of this as a piece of writing?'

'I must say,' said Phyllis, 'I can't help thinking it's a bit unnecessary.'

'A bit unnecessary,' said Quinn. 'That's rather crushing, Phyllis. Would you care to elaborate?'

'Sordid,' said Phyllis. 'And that's my last word on the subject.'

'It left my sea frozen too, I'm afraid,' said Jill.

'Perhaps detachment was precisely what Jake was aiming for,' mused Quinn.

'That was so detached it was in outer space,' said Jill. 'Or was he being ironic? Perhaps he was being ironic.'

'Of course I was being fucking ironic,' said Jake crossly. 'Everything's ironic now. Hadn't you noticed? Especially sex. I mean, look at what Nadia's wearing, just look at that for an example, it's very nice, all those strategic zips, but she's trying to make a fool of me as a red-blooded heterosexual male. Aren't you, love. You're being ironic, aren't you.'

'What?' said Nadia.

'Take no notice of him,' whispered Marion, on her other side.

'This mock-simplicity,' continued Jill, 'this wide-eyed use of the present tense, it's so offensively *knowing*, don't you think?'

'I suppose you're all for naive self-expression,' sneered Jake. 'Spreading you and yours out naked on the page. But literature's not about that, it's not bloody therapy, is it. That's not what it's about.'

'It can be that too, of course,' said Quinn.

'You have to go to the opera now for anything straight-forward,' continued Jill. 'I mean, what's so clever about putting quotation marks round everything? Happy campers, I'm sick of them. So defended. Self-defensive. Take your box off, Jake.'

'From the piece he's just read us, I rather thought he had,' said Quinn mildly. 'Now, did anyone manage to include a mirror? To follow the exercise? It's perfectly all right not to, of course, but – ah, Marion. Please.'

Marion cleared her throat several times, fell into a brief violent attack of coughing which necessitated thuds on the back from Jill, beside her, followed by a purple-faced pantomime with hand movements signifying that she would be fully recovered in a minute. Her story, when it emerged, concerned a woman in late middle age, like herself, getting ready for an anniversary meal with her husband, her reflection in the new blue dress (mirror), his favourite scent; the phone call from his secretary saying he'd been held up in a meeting, the sense of déjà vu (oxymoron), the gin-and-tonics (oxymoron); the time ticking by, the next two phone calls, both from the secretary again, and again the delay, fermenting rage (oxymoron), until at last the late arrival of the husband, his raised eyebrow at her jealous imaginings, his plausible explanation (reversal of fortune), the fond last words, 'Silly bitch.'

'You have skill,' said Quinn. 'You have sensitivity. I particularly liked the gin-and-tonic's miserable sparkle. But the ending was a cop-out. As I think you realize.'

'Yes,' said Marion, surprised.

'I wanted you to exercise more psychological insight,' continued Quinn. 'You may not have psychological insight, of course, though I suspect you do. Now, the secretary is very interesting. She is the mediator of these lies.'

'Lies?' said Marion.

'What the teller of this story needs to know is,' said Quinn, 'Is the man having an affair with his secretary? Or is he a busy man who likes going to meetings? I want you to probe the wound. Stick your fingers in it. Explore.'

'Yes,' said Marion. 'I do see.'

'Next?' said Quinn.

Don moved into action at last. Silently he handed round xeroxed copies to each member of the group, and then, without once lifting his eyes, he began to read. It took a good quarter of an hour. Nadia looked around her discreetly, incredulously, as his voice droned on, but the others seemed utterly resigned. Phyllis was dozing lightly, as was Jill, while Karen was applying top coat to her nails under cover of her handbag. Jake and Marion were busily writing. Quinn stared at the ceiling.

As far as Nadia could tell, Don's story was a chapter from a longer narrative involving a race of dwarfish mead-drinking men with names like Mope and Clench speaking in lofty sci-fi dialect, and there was something to do with a maiden, beautiful but dangerous, who lived in a mountain and had a mysterious crimson mouth which unfortunately showed long sharp teeth when she smiled. The narrative stopped abruptly, with Don collecting his copies, again in silence.

'Thank you, Don,' said Quinn courteously. 'That seems to be coming along nicely.'

Don stared at the table and writhed, letting slip a quick smile as though he were dealing a playing card, gone before it was seen.

'Now,' said Quinn. 'Time for coffee, I think.'

Rousing themselves, they drifted off towards the drinks machine in the lobby, and soon each was cradling a plastic cup of something brown. They coalesced into little knots in the stairwell, beside the noticeboard, anywhere to be out of the draught. Don sloped out into the night with a furtive backward glance and another fugitive smile.

'Oh look,' said Nadia to Jake, who was at her elbow. 'Poor man, is he all right?'

'He's fine,' Jake reassured her. 'He's read his piece, he's had his reaction. Well, no, not quite that, was it. No. He's had a room full of quiet people while he droned on about his wee men. That's why he comes.'

'Oh,' said Nadia, looking at Jake warily.

'He always does it,' said Jake. 'Honest! Makes sure he reads just before the break, shoots his bolt, then he doesn't have to sit through the second half.'

Nadia smiled at last.

'So what do you write?' she said.

'Poetry mainly. Novels when I can, but I feel increasingly that the novel is finished. I'm about to go into TV, that's why I've been coming along, I want to get Quinn interested in co-scripting with me.'

'Have you had a novel published?' asked Nadia, preparing to be dazzled.

'Not as yet,' said Jake moodily. 'It's difficult. I'd have been published years ago if I'd been a woman.'

'Why?' said Nadia.

'Oh come on,' said Jake. 'It's a piece of piss these days if you're a woman. Do you know, you have the most delirious eyes, your right one's even bluer than the left. A sort of drenched violet.'

'Oh,' said Nadia. She savoured the drenched violet. It was different, anyway.

'I'll tell you a secret, Nadia,' Jake whispered thrillingly, funnily, crinkling his eyes. 'I'll tell you why women writers are on a hiding to nowhere. They can't cut the mustard. They lack attack. The appetite for cut and thrust. They just aren't nasty enough, or if they are anyone with any sense avoids them like the plague. Or they end up writing about wombs, like big Jill over there. Or abandonment, by which I mean being ditched rather than the cheerful sort. Or gay, of course. Which I hope you're not. Because *I* want you.'

Nadia gasped. It was like being chatted up by a creature from another age, a unicorn or perhaps a pterodactyl, she had never heard anything quite like it; he was talking rubbish of course but the last bit was quite punchy.

'Better be a muse than a writer,' persisted Jake. 'Be *my* muse. I need a muse.'

'*Je m'amuse avec ma muse,*' said Quinn, appearing between them noiselessly. 'The trouble is, Nadia, you walk in beauty like the night and your fabulous garments will create excitement wherever you go, but don't let him persuade you that those are good enough reasons for being rather than doing. If doing is what you want to do.'

'I want to write,' said Nadia.

'Then write,' said Quinn.

'I wanted to write when I was your age,' said Jill, just back from her phone call to the babysitter. 'I was at university so I went along to a creative writing group, walked in a bit late, sat at the back, and the line they were pondering was, "Turning slowly in her cunt." All boys except me. I stayed a little while but I felt, well . . .'

'A bit of a cunt,' suggested Jake.

'Right on, Jake,' she said. 'That must have been twenty years ago, when I was a mere slip of a thing and you were in your heyday. Come on, Nadia, come and meet the girls.'

'It's a waste of time,' Karen was saying as she drained her coffee. 'I haven't written anything good on this course. He's pathetic. I'm packing it in.' She dropped her halffiinished cigarette and ground it into the tiles with her Doc Marten.

'I feel I may fall out with that young man,' said Phyllis. 'I hope he doesn't come next week.'

'Young?' said Jill. 'He's fifty if he's a day.'

'Even so, dear,' said Phyllis. 'If you'll make my excuses to Quinn, I think I'll go home early to bed.'

'My trouble is,' yawned Jill, once they had gone, 'I'm so tired I can only write about how tired I am.'

'Is Milly still waking?' asked Marion.

'At two and at five,' said Jill.

'I liked your womb poem last week,' said Marion.

'Oh did you?' said Jill, surprised. 'I hadn't realized it was one, you know, until Quinn pointed it out. I thought it was about sleep.'

'How many have you got?' asked Nadia.

'What, poems?' said Jill. 'Oh no, children. Three. No, I don't really approve of womb poems.'

'Why not?' said Marion. 'We have our wisdom.'

'Oh, come off it,' said Jill. 'You make us sound hand-knitted.'

'My friend Lorna's going to have a baby,' said Nadia. 'She says she feels, like, totally different since she got pregnant. More in touch with herself. It's amazing, she says.'

'Yes, well,' said Jill. 'But I'm not having any of that stuff about men having the brains while women get the Knowledge of Nature. Babies as consolation prizes. That's just back to square one. Has your friend Lorna got a man?'

'No,' said Nadia. 'He said get rid of it but she didn't want to. So he went.'

'I couldn't ever write like Jake,' mused Marion. 'I just couldn't do it. I can see it's very clever, you know, but it's too exhausting, the way he uses words, so forced, he bashes away like a pile driver. I mean, we, women, we're able to be sexual even if we're not actually, you know, it's not all just *sex*, it's eating, it's drawing the curtains, it's, you know, even the way we're just standing here, *being* . . .'

'Marion, you're havering,' said Jill. 'Your main trouble is, if you want to know, since you can't be the top dog, you'll be the nice dog.'

'But I don't think of myself as a dog,' said Marion. 'I mean, if the man is a dog, then I'm a cat.'

'What?' said Jill. 'A different species now, are we?'

'That's what a lot of my friends are saying,' said Marion.

'And mine,' said Nadia.

Back round the library table, Quinn said, 'Do I sense a new binary fission at work within my shrunken class? A certain grimness? A *froideur*? Perhaps we should tell some jokes. A proper joke, please, or a funny story, but pay attention to your timing. Three minutes to prepare.'

'No, I can't tell jokes,' said Marion. 'I'm sorry. I've tried. I always fluff the punch-line.'

'The punch-line,' said Quinn. 'Yes, the punch-line. Supposedly an exclusively male affair. A woman's approach is traditionally more holistic and gentle.'

'They always want us to be *nicer* than them,' fumed Jill.

'We are,' said Marion.

'That's not the point,' snarled Jill. 'Anyway, I can be funny. Bloody funny.'

'No you can't,' said Jake. 'Everybody knows there have

only been about three funny women in the history of the world, and you're not one of them.'

'There is usually something aggressive or critical behind any joke,' mused Quinn.

'I tell jokes with my friends,' said Nadia. 'But not with men around.'

'How accurate do you think this sort of sheep-and-goats business is?' asked Quinn. 'This sort of gender categorization? I ask this with an open mind as I really don't know what I think here. I've tended to take refuge in the idea of androgyny, but I can see that's just pussyfooting about, really.'

'What do you mean, gender categorization?' said Marion.

'I mean, for example, do you think it's fair to say, as I have heard observed recently, that women have a better eye for detail than men?'

'Oh, yes, definitely,' said Marion. 'My husband's always saying I can't see further than the end of my nose. But then that's only natural, on the whole we've had to stay indoors more than men. Up till recently. What with the housework and the rapists.'

'So the horizon was rarely further than ten feet,' mused Quinn. 'Yes. I can see how that might develop an eye for detail.'

'Shall I tell my joke about the old whore sucking oranges?' said Jake.

'If you do, I'll tell my one about the shark and the nude male swimmer,' said Nadia.

'Attagirl,' said Jill.

'I also want you to consider,' said Quinn, 'whether it is

any longer possible for thoughtful women to write traditional heterosexual love stories.'

'What?' said Nadia.

'Why ever not?' said Marion.

'Because of having to write within the patriarchal
tradition, he means,' said Jill. 'You know, she sank into his
arms, all that sort of stuff.'

'Then she ended up with her arms in his sink,' said
Nadia, with a happy laugh.

'Yes, I think I've heard that one before too,' said Quinn.

'It depends on what you mean by thoughtful,' said Jill.

'I suppose I must mean feminist,' said Quinn. 'Although
I hesitate to use the word as I'm not sure of its definition.'

'The trouble is, neither am I,' said Jill. 'There is no
manifesto. As far as I can see, it can mean, unless you're
gay you're a traitor, or it can mean you'd like some help
with the washing up. Or anything in between.'

'I don't really mind, so long as they're pretty,' said Jake.

'What a wag,' said Jill. 'What I don't agree with, though,
is this new tendency automatically to assign the sensitive,
sensuous twisty-twiny stuff to the feminine principle
while all the wit and drive goes to the masculine.'

'Think of Henry James,' said Quinn. 'Proust. What could
be more tendril-like than their prose?'

'This attempt to make out that women's writing is like
laying an egg,' said Jill. 'Or knitting. Why so for women
more than for men? If you prick us, do we not bleed?'

'Sorry?' said Jake.

'I like short sentences,' she continued, ignoring him. 'I'm
very direct, I admire Hemingway. Where does that leave
me?'

'Perhaps – have you considered? – that in your writing you're doing male impersonation?' asked Quinn.

'That's a wife-beating question if ever there was one,' said Jill. 'And I suppose you'd say Proust and Henry James wrote in drag.'

'What are you talking about?' said Nadia, utterly baffled.

'She's talking *cojones*,' said Jake.

'Why do I have to be water and earth?' asked Jill wildly. 'Why can't I be air and fire?'

'Are you a Pisces?' said Marion. 'I thought so.'

'Yes, but what if I was an Aries?' cried Jill. 'Some women are.'

'Aries isn't air, is he?' said Nadia.

'Oh, you know what I mean,' snapped Jill.

'He's a ram,' said Nadia.

'Who's a ram,' said Jake.

Nadia giggled.

'It's a curious thing,' said Quinn, 'but I find I can fit any description in the horoscope's personality. Bold, sanguine, earthy, full of leadership qualities; yes, I say, that's me. Then, romantic, sensitive, idealistic, unworldly; that's me too. Which reminds me of an ancient Chinese oracle game I know. Let's play it now, we've got time.'

'I'd have said you were an Aquarius, Quinn,' said Marion. 'Or even a Virgo.'

'My birthday is a secret,' said Quinn. 'Now. Let the oracle be this fur-lined glove. Hail, mighty oracle! We must present the oracle with a genuine question. Be thinking what this might be. Before presenting the question we are going to surround it with flimflam, close our eyes, bow three times, burn incense if we have any, recite some incantatory mumbo-jumbo, process once round the table while humming through the left nostril, and then, only then, present the question.'

'So where will the answer come from?' asked Nadia.

'It will come from beneath the oracle, from the dictionary upon which the oracle is resting. One of us will place a finger, blind, on a page, any page, a definition, any definition – and the answer will be somewhere there, within the definition. It never fails. The synapses are just waiting to cling on. You'll see.'

'I think the question should be about Nadia,' said Jake. 'What's going to happen to Nadia?'

'Yes, Nadia's the youngest,' said Marion. 'She's got it all ahead of her.'

'Yes,' said Jill. 'What should Nadia do next?'

'Nadia's future,' said Quinn.

Soon they were performing the invented rituals, lighting cigarettes, chanting, stumbling into each other with their eyes closed, until at last Quinn ordered them, sonorous and mock-priestly, to be still.

'Tell us, O mighty Oracle,' he addressed the glove. 'Pray tell us, what does the future hold for our young friend?'

He lifted the glove reverently, placed it on Nadia's folded hands, then, with a flourish, closed his eyes, flung open the dictionary and struck the page with his index finger.

'You must read it now, aloud to all of us,' he instructed Nadia.

'Generative, a,' read Nadia. 'Of procreation; able to produce, productive; – grammar, set of rules whereby permissible sentences may be generated from elements of a language.'

'Well,' said Quinn, and gave a broad smile.

'Books,' said Jill, as Jake said, 'Babies.'

'Generative,' said Quinn, 'I like that word. "Generative warmth", now where's that from?'

'Copy it down, dear,' said Marion. 'I think it may be a sign.'

'But what does it *mean*?' said Nadia.

'The oracle has spoken,' said Quinn. 'And pretty clearly, too, for an oracle. As Marion suggested, you should record the definition, then you can think about its meaning later.'

'I can't find it,' said Nadia, starting to search her many zipped pockets.

'Here,' said Jake. 'Borrow mine.'

'No thanks,' said Nadia, waving her pen triumphantly. 'Here it is!'

'Now,' said Quinn. 'Time for a drink.'